NO TIME FOR GUILT

"You're far more my type than Renee. I've known that a long time," Trent said.

"What type am I?"

"The type who thinks a good time is a drive in the country and a nice slow dance, among other things."

I looked at him and smiled. His hand lifted my chin, and he leaned over to kiss me. Before our lips ever met, my body was on fire. When our skin touched, I felt his warm, moist, eager lips match mine. I pulled away, took his face in my hands, and let myself look deep into those tender eyes. I wanted him to see what I was feeling. For a little while I forgot he was going with my best friend and lost myself in loving someone new.

Other Avon Flare Books by
Jeanette Mines

ANOTHER CHANCE
RECKLESS

RISKING IT

Jeanette Mines

AN AVON FLARE BOOK

AVON BOOKS
A division of
The Hearst Corporation
105 Madison Avenue
New York, New York 10016

Copyright © 1988 by Jeanette Mines
Published by arrangement with the author
Library of Congress Catalog Card Number: 87-91634
ISBN: 0-380-75401-0
RL: 4.6

First Avon Flare Printing: February 1988

AVON FLARE TRADEMARK REG. U.S. PAT. OFF. AND IN OTHER COUNTRIES, MARCA REGISTRADA, HECHO EN U.S.A.

Printed in the U.S.A.

K-R   10   9   8   7   6   5   4   3   2

For my wonderful daughter,
Marie Ryan

Chapter 1

The night before the first day of my senior year I hardly slept at all. Excited because I had finally made it to my last year of high school and determined to make the most of the next nine months, I tossed and turned and woke up frequently.

The alarm jerked me from a dream about Sam Benson, my first and only true love. The incessant beeping rescued me from the frustration I always feel when images of Sam haunt my sleep.

In the hospital after the accident, I dreamed about him often. I don't much anymore. This dream didn't surprise me, though. Since Sam and I had met on my very first day of high school, this time of year always evokes strong memories of our short time together.

I don't think about Sam a lot anymore. Oh, I still keep in my dresser drawer the picture of him I cut out of the yearbook, but a long time ago I purged my room of the few mementos I had of our time together. One afternoon after I came home from the hospital, I got furious at Sam's senseless death and threw the crumbled red and gold leaves we had collected that fall into a garbage can. Then I tossed in a lit match and watched the leaves curl into flames and turn to ash. I felt a lot better after that.

1

The fire escape rope ladder, the only present Sam ever gave me, is buried in the back of my closet. I bring it out every once in a while when I feel lonely. A couple of times Mom suggested I throw it away, but I refuse to part with it.

After I awoke from my dream about Sam, I flipped on the radio and dragged myself out of bed. In the shower I reminded myself of the vow I had made to put the past behind me and make my senior year special. Maybe I'd even try dating a little more. Just because I'd had some bummer dates since Sam died, didn't mean I had to give up on boys completely.

I dressed quickly and started on my hair. Renee was coming extra early to pick me up so we could swing by Arly's before school. Arly's is the unofficial senior hangout and each year on the first day of school all the new seniors gather there. Somehow Renee had conned her mom into relinquishing the station wagon for the day so we could have our own wheels this morning.

When she honked, I grabbed my bag and ran out the kitchen door. I stopped dead when I saw Renee leaning against a powder-blue Mustang. Her grin told me all.

"Fantastic!" I screamed as I circled the new car.

"Isn't it the greatest?" Renee held up the keys. "All mine. Do you believe it?"

"Wow! It's perfect."

When Renee's boyfriend Brian left for college, so did her chauffeur. For the last month Renee had begged for a car on a daily basis, but we both thought her pleading was in vain. I was delighted to see that her parents had succumbed to the pressure. I slid into the navy-blue velour passenger seat.

"Why didn't you tell me?"

2

"I wanted to surprise you. It was worth it, too. You should have seen your face when you saw it."

"I'm in shock. What a way to start the year!"

Renee stepped on the accelerator and eased the car onto the street.

Renee's joy made me smile. Ever since early August when Brian left for football training camp, Renee had practically been living at my house and feeling pretty miserable. Renee and Brian had been together for three years, and she couldn't imagine senior year without him. I couldn't either. Since freshman year I had kidded her about her busy social life, but lately there wasn't much to tease her about. I hoped now that school was starting and she had a new car she'd be a little happier. As much as I gave her a hard time about her full social calendar, I kind of liked it. She often insisted I join her and Brian, and if it hadn't been for them I might have sat home a lot more than I did.

Not that I don't go out. I've had a few disastrous dates since Sam died, and a couple that were passable. Last month I went to a movie with Tim Murphy and actually enjoyed myself a little. But mostly I go places alone or with Renee and Brian. Nobody is as intriguing as Sam was. Jeb, who was Sam's best friend, claims I'm too fussy. I don't agree. Maybe I'm just afraid of getting hurt again. One loss in life is plenty for anybody.

"Don't you look good today." Renee inspected me from head to toe. "Those hoops are perfect with that belt."

I was wearing the two-inch gold earrings Mom had brought me from St. Paul last month. The wide gold belt was a birthday present my brother Tom had sent from college. I figured his girlfriend picked it out.

3

"You don't look so bad yourself." Renee's Guess shirt and jeans looked spectacular with her Gucci boots and shoulder bag. "Your mom came through on your last shopping spree, I see."

Renee had invited me to go shopping with her in the city, but I declined. It was too depressing trying to stretch my limited budget when shopping with Renee. She assumed her parents had an endless supply of money just to keep her closets bulging.

"She sure did. I hit Daytons at full throttle."

"I can see that. Good thing your parents are so generous. What will you do if Brian doesn't make a lot of money?"

"I'm not worried. You know Brian. Nothing but the best."

I laughed. She was right. Brian liked expensive things as much as Renee. He'd make sure he landed a job with real potential.

"And if he doesn't, I'll just have to find someone who can."

"You know, Renee, that's the second time this week you've mentioned finding someone else. What's going on with you? You and Brian have a fight or something?"

"Not really, but I think one's brewing. He called again last night and he sounded real strange."

"Like how?"

"I don't know. Something's bothering him, but I can't figure out what."

"Maybe he's worried about football."

"I doubt it. He says practice is a killer, but he'll survive. Nothing like a little competition to get his blood pumping. No, it's something else. He even suggested maybe I shouldn't come for his first game this weekend."

4

"But for months you've been planning to go for the Labor Day weekend."

"I know. Maybe he's just nervous. Or maybe it's me. This not having a boyfriend around is the pits. Jeannie, I don't know how you do it."

"You don't have to have a boyfriend around to be happy, Renee."

"For you, maybe, but not for me. This last month I've been so lonely."

"I know it's hard, Renee. But it'll get easier."

"I'm not sure about that. But I do know I'm sick of football. This summer that's all Brian talked about. And then he was on that goofy eating kick to put on weight. I think I put on more pounds than he did."

"You look fine." Renee constantly battled her weight. Sugar and chocolate were her downfall.

"What difference does it make? Who's going to care? Oh, Jeannie, I'm so tired of him being gone. This is my last year of high school. I hate this. I want to have fun."

"And you will. Wait and see. Maybe you should think about dating other people."

"Brian and I talked about it once. But he said he couldn't stand the thought of me being with someone else. And I can't stand thinking about him with anyone else, either. The only problem is, I'm bored to death. He's off to college having a grand time and I'm suppose to sit here and wait for him. I don't like it."

"Of course you don't. It's got to be hard for you not having him around. You two were *always* together."

"For three whole years. And now he's gone and I'm supposed to be content to see him once a month, if I'm lucky. Brian is so wrapped up in football that he doesn't realize what I'm going through. And this business about not wanting me to come for his first game doesn't make sense. I wish I knew why he sounded so strange when he called."

"I bet he's just as miserable as you are. I'm sure he hates not having you there. You'll have a great weekend once you're together again. You'll see."

"I hope you're right. My problem is I like to have a good time *all* the time."

Renee maneuvered her way into Arly's parking lot and pulled into a no-parking zone directly in front of the entrance.

"Here, get me a Coke." She handed me a dollar. "I'll join you if I can find a place to park."

"A Coke for breakfast?"

"I know I shouldn't, but I need it. I'm having sugar withdrawal."

Arly's was jammed with kids. Jeb was near the front of the line. I snuck in behind him.

"Hey, Jeannie, how's it going?"

"Good, Jeb. Look at you with the new haircut. You almost look normal."

"Oh no, the ultimate insult." Jeb's stringy blond hair had flirted with his collar ever since freshman year. This new clean-cut look was hard to get used to.

"One more year, huh kid, then we're out. Hard to believe, isn't it?"

"It sure is. I hope it's a good one." The waitress shoved Jeb's food in a bag, and I ordered Renee's Coke and a croissant for me.

Just then Renee cut in line beside me.

"I see you got some new wheels," Jeb said to her.

"Yeah. Isn't it great?" I answered, hoping Renee

6

and Jeb weren't going to start in on each other. Not this early in the day.

"I hate to admit it, but that *is* a classy car. I wish my old man was loaded."

"And sober," Renee whispered to me. I shot her my nastiest look. If she mentioned Jeb's dad's drinking problem out loud, I'd wring her neck.

"You say something?" Jeb asked.

"Nothing important. Glad you like the car. I'll see you outside, Jeannie." Renee grabbed her Coke, scooted under the rope, and disappeared out the door. She really didn't like being around Jeb for long.

"I'll never understand it, Jeannie, never." Jeb shook his head.

"You mean Renee and me being friends?"

"That's right. You two are so opposite."

"That's probably why we get along so well. Funny, she says the same thing about you and me."

"I'll bet she does. How's she surviving without the jock?"

"She misses him."

"She'll replace him within a week. Mark my words."

"Come on, Jeb. Give me a break. Renee's my friend."

"I know. I'm just teasing. I've got to go. See you in the sweatpen." Jeb grabbed his breakfast and headed for the door.

When I found where Renee had parked the Mustang, she wasn't in the car. Just like her to disappear and make us late the first day. I was finishing my croissant when she slid into the driver's seat.

"I knew this car was going to bring me luck, and it has already." She rolled down her window and dumped her Coke on the ground.

"What are you doing?"

"Don't turn around now. But three cars over is the most gorgeous guy you have ever laid eyes on, and that beautiful hunk of man is about to enroll at our school."

"Where?" I tried to see who she was talking about, but I couldn't get a good look.

"With Rich Dravis. Can you see him?"

"No."

"Well, you will at school. His name is Trent Justin and if he's anything like his face, this year is going to be terrific, *just terrific.*"

I threw her the funniest look.

"Oh, sorry. It just came out," she said.

"It's okay. It's just weird hearing those words again." Sam had nicknamed me J.T. He said it stood for "Just Terrific." A sudden sense of loneliness jabbed me in the chest. Would that feeling ever go away?

"He's that gorgeous, huh?"

"He certainly is. And that's just what we need. Someone new to add a little excitement to this place. What a hunk! Wait till you see him."

"You sound pretty interested. Are you that worried about Brian?"

"Not really. But just because I'm committed to Brian doesn't mean I can't look, does it?"

"Of course not."

"Oh, look, they're pulling out. You ready?"

Renee squealed out of Arly's and cut in front of two cars trying to maneuver a position behind Rich in the high school parking lot. But the lot was jammed, and Rich found a single space on the south side near the main door. By the time Renee parked her car, Rich and the new kid were already in the building.

"Darn, they got away. I wonder where they went. No doubt to the Circle. Meet you there in a few minutes. I want to see my counselor."

"Okay." Renee scurried through the crowd, and I wandered toward the Circle. Tradition calls for the new seniors to gather in the courtyard for a class rally on the first day of school. It was hard to believe this year I was one of those seniors.

The Circle was already mobbed. Kids milled everywhere. One boy had climbed a tree and was pulling confetti from a box and letting it drift over the crowd. Another guy, the unofficial class clown, had donned the tiger mascot uniform and was trying to organize the chaos. No one paid much attention.

The ringing of the first bell was the signal. The crowd quieted, and when the bell stopped the roar of the seniors began. For a full minute, 300 senior voices cheered and chanted, "Senior Power! Senior Privileges! Senioritis! Seniormightis!"

When the chanting ceased, the tiger mascot led us all in one final cheer and then on cue the entire senior class began the school song.

As the song ended and the crowd started to disperse, sounds like shots rang out. An eerie silence descended, and then another round of bangs filled the air.

"It's a gun. He's got a gun," someone shouted. Everyone pushed for the exit at the same time. It was a mob scene. I felt myself crushed in the crowd. I was tripping over the people in front of me.

When I tried to turn, another round of explosions sounded. The crowd crushed tighter against the door. I stumbled and fell. I couldn't get up. There wasn't room. Someone stepped on my hand. Somebody else went right over my back. Fear of being trampled to death overpowered me as I lay frozen on the ground. Then I felt a hand under my elbow. Someone was lifting me to my feet. When I was almost upright, arms encircled my shoulders and someone half-carried, half-dragged me to the side of the building and lowered me to the ground.

"Put your head between your knees and breathe deeply."

I obeyed without question.

Gradually my breathing returned to normal. I started to lift my head.

"Not yet. You still look pretty pale."

I didn't recognize the voice. All I could see was my rescuer's brown hand-tooled cowboy boots and new jeans. When I eventually looked up, he was looking toward the kid in the tree, then he turned to me. "That little sucker is firing a starter gun. That's all. Just a starter gun. Sure did sound real, though."

I looked toward the tree, then at the quizzical look on the face of the guy in front of me. Deep dimples, sky-blue eyes, and jet-black hair combined with his tanned, smooth skin made a striking profile. I smiled.

He grinned and stuck out his hand. "I'm Trent Justin."

I took his warm hand in mine. His grip was firm, yet gentle. "I'm Jeannie Tanger."

An announcement over the loudspeaker summoned everyone to homeroom. The principal stood at the base of the tree motioning for the kid with the fake gun to climb down.

"Let me help you." Trent reached down and took my arm. He lifted me to my feet.

"Thanks," I mumbled. His hand on my arm was soft and warm, yet strong. I didn't want to think

10

about how foolish I must have looked sprawled on the ground.

"Nice meeting you." He smiled. His dimples deepened and then he was gone.

I watched him walk away, then hurried to my homeroom. What an embarrassing way to meet the new guy in school. But in his smooth, gentle manner, he had made an awkward situation seem easy. Renee was right. He was gorgeous.

Renee wasn't at her locker for fourth-hour lunch, so I went to the cafeteria without her. Apparently she had a new schedule, so we weren't going to have the same lunch period. I didn't really mind. Renee loved to flit around the cafeteria and socialize. I preferred to eat quickly and then relax in the Circle.

All the confetti was gone and the Circle was back to normal. Everyone was laughing about the fake gun. Rumor had it the kid in the tree was in big trouble for creating such a panic.

After school Renee was sitting on the hood of her Mustang when I got to the parking lot.

"Guess who's in my physics class?" she called as soon as I was in hearing distance.

"From that smile on your face it isn't too hard to figure out. But since when are you taking physics?"

"Since my father told my counselor I had to. That's what I wanted to see my counselor about, but she wouldn't let me out of the class. Now that I've seen who's in the class, I don't mind as much."

"I assume we're talking about Trent Justin."

"Yep. And, speak of the devil."

Trent and Rich were walking right toward us.

"Hi, Rich. How's it going?" Renee flashed them her brightest smile. What's she up to? I thought.

11

"Renee, how you doing? I like your wheels." Rich walked around the car inspecting every detail. Trent hesitated.

"Hey, Trent, you met Renee this morning, remember? And that's Jeannie Tanger," Rich said, motioning to me.

Trent glanced at me and nodded. I nodded back.

"So you're new here, huh?" Renee moved right in.

"Yeah, came from the city."

"What do you think so far?"

"Not bad. Everybody is real friendly."

"We sure are. Going to be at Arly's tonight?"

"I don't know. I hadn't thought about it."

"Oh, do come. Everyone will be there," Renee insisted.

"He'll come. I'll make sure of that," Rich said. "How's Brian doing at State?"

"Who knows? I haven't seen him for a month. Football, you know. His first game's Saturday. I'm going to see him play."

"Well, tell him hello. We sure do miss him here. Our team stinks without the guys from last year."

"Do you play football?" Renee asked Trent.

"A little."

"He's being modest. He's terrific. In fact, that's where we're headed now. You know how Coach is. Can't stand it if we're one minute late."

"Well, good luck. We'll cheer for you. Won't we, Jeannie?"

"Sure." I wished I could think of something to say, but my mind was a blank. He wasn't looking at me anyway, so why did I care? He sure was looking Renee over, though. And he flashed her that gorgeous smile. I wanted him to do that to me.

12

When the boys disappeared around the building, we jumped in the Mustang.

"Isn't he something?" Renee said.

"He sure is. And I'm sure your interest in him is purely platonic." I sounded more sarcastic than I'd intended, but Renee didn't seem to notice.

"Of course. Like I said this morning, a girl can look, can't she?"

"Sure," I answered. But she was doing more than looking, and we both knew it.

Chapter 2

The first week of school passed quickly. The teachers loaded on the work. Wanted to break us in right, they said. Get us ready for college. So between my job at the car wash and my homework, I didn't have much free time.

On Saturday, the combination gas station and car wash where I worked was mobbed. Mr. Nolan, the owner, was running a promotion. When a customer bought ten gallons of gas, a car wash was half-price. My job was to sit in a little glass booth, collect money for gas, and give out car wash passes. If someone wanted just a car wash, he paid the supervisor at the head of the line.

Every couple of hours the supervisor brought me the money he had collected. I'd count it and drop it into the safe buried in the floor beneath me.

By evening, I was exhausted. Renee was at State visiting Brian for the weekend and wasn't coming back until Monday. Mom and Dad were at a friend's cookout. I flipped on the television and plopped on the couch.

About nine o'clock the phone rang.

"Hi."

"Hi," I answered. I didn't recognize the voice. "Who is this?"

"It's me. Renee."

"Renee? It doesn't sound like you. What's wrong? Where are you?"

"At the truck stop outside of town. I don't want to go home. Can I come over?" Once she started talking I realized she'd been crying. She sounded on the verge of tears again.

"Of course. You don't have to ask."

"Are you alone?"

"Yeah, the folks are out."

"Good. I couldn't be sociable now."

A few minutes later her car pulled into the driveway. When I opened the door, she took one look at me and started crying.

"Brian, right?" I gently pulled her into the house and guided her to the couch in the living room.

She nodded yes, but couldn't talk.

I let her cry for a while and then handed her a tissue. "Okay, now tell me what happened."

"He's a two-faced phony! That's what he is. Nothing but a spineless jerk," she said, wiping her face.

I waited for her to continue.

"You know his big song and dance about us being faithful and true and his big plan that we should wait for each other? Well, that's all it was. Big-time talk by the big-time college man. Seems it took him all of two weeks to find a replacement for me."

"Brian has a girlfriend?"

"Yes, and he didn't even have the guts to tell me. I had to make a total fool of myself before I found out."

"What happened?"

"I went down there. That was my first mistake."

"I gathered that, but tell me the details."

"Remember I told you he was acting real weird about me coming this weekend, even though we had planned on it for months? Well, on Thursday night he called and said he'd be nervous with me there and said maybe I shouldn't come. I told him nervous or not, I would be there. What a crock that story was! I've seen him play dozens of games. Never bothered him before. All of a sudden he's nervous. The only thing he was nervous about was me finding out about Sandy."

"Sandy?"

"Yeah, that's her name. Tall, thin blonde who thinks he's just so adorable."

"How do you know?"

"She told me."

"She did? You actually met her?"

"Let me start from the beginning. All last night I sensed something was wrong. When I got there, instead of going out, we sat in his room and watched TV. Hardly made out, anything. Here I haven't seen him for a month and I get the cold-shoulder treatment. About 9:30, I suggested we go out and get something to eat, and Brian said he couldn't go out because he had a game the next day."

"That makes sense."

"You're as gullible as I am. I believed him, too. But I found out later other football players went out. The only restriction was that they be in by 10:30."

"What was going on, then? Sandy?"

"You got it. And this afternoon it all came out. There was a postgame picnic planned by some guys in the dorm. Everyone was talking about how much fun it was going to be. But after the game Brian decided he didn't want to go. He said he was tired and was sure it would be a real drag. The only drag about it was that Brian was afraid to take me.''

''But you went anyway?''

''You bet. I told Brian that if he was tired he could rest and meet me there later. I hadn't come for the weekend to spend it sitting in the dorm. Finally he agreed to go, and what a mistake! I knew something was wrong when Brian introduced me as an old family friend from home who came to see his game. Never once did he call me his girlfriend.''

''You must have been furious.''

''At first I didn't get it. I'm so dumb sometimes I amaze myself. But I got it real quick when he asked me to get him something to eat. When I came back, this girl was hanging all over Brian. And when I walked up to them, Brian turned red and tried to get her away from him. But she didn't budge. Finally Brian introduced us.''

''Family friend again?''

''That's right. Spineless Brian introduced us and then asked me to get him a beer. Like a fool I did. The whole time I was in line at the keg I watched him talking to her. She kept looking at him and smiling. I just wanted to throw up. But somehow he managed to get her away from him by the time I got back with his beer. And before I could ask him about her he said he needed catsup for his hamburger. He left me standing there all alone. I felt like such a jerk. Then this girl comes back and starts talking to me. She acted like it was the most natural thing in the world for her to be there. Said how nice it was of me to come for the game.''

''What did you say to her?''

''Not much. She did all the talking. Chatted about what a great game it was. About how well they all played, especially Brian. That's when she says to me, 'Isn't he the most adorable guy? These past two weeks with Brian have been like a dream.' "

"She didn't say that?"

"She sure did. I choked on my Coke. Then it finally dawned on me. Why he didn't want me at his game. Why he didn't want to come to the picnic. The whole bit. I was so furious and hurt I couldn't talk. I just stood there while she rattled on about Brian and how much fun he was. Then she said she couldn't believe he didn't have a girlfriend back home. Cute guy like him."

"Are you kidding me?"

"I wish I were. It was awful. Just then Brian came back, took one look at the two of us together, and suggested he show me the campus. I told him I'd seen enough of the campus already. Then I took the beer he was holding, poured it over his head, and told Sandy now she could believe him. He didn't have a girlfriend back home *anymore*."

"What did Brian do?"

"Nothing. He stood there like a complete jerk."

"What about Sandy?"

"In that sickening sweet voice, she said, 'What's she talking about, Brian?' And he still just stood there. That's when I yanked off the ring he gave me last Christmas and flung it at him."

"Oh, Renee. How terrible."

"Then with all the dignity I could muster, I turned and walked off. You should have seen the crowds part when I did that. And here I am. No ring, no boyfriend, no dignity. I'll never, ever be able to show my face on that campus again."

"Hey, I like your style. I'm sure a lot of the kids did too."

"I doubt it. They're probably still laughing."

"Only at Brian. He's the one who made a real fool of himself."

"I can't believe he'd do that to me. Drop me just like that after three years. What am I going to do?"

Tears welled in Renee's eyes, and she started crying all over again. From the bathroom I brought her a wet washcloth and towel.

"Here, wash your face. You'll feel better. Have you eaten?"

She shook her head no.

"Then let's order a pizza. I'm starved myself. I'll call Nick's. They deliver."

Renee washed her face while I called.

"What about your folks? Do they know you're home?"

"No. They think I'm with Brian, and I'd just as soon keep it that way."

"You can stay here tonight, then. Mom and Dad won't be home until late. We'll have pizza, watch a late movie, and talk. What do you say? Tomorrow we'll figure out what to do. I think you've had enough for one day."

"I'd like that. The thought of having to face my mother and tell her about Brian is too much."

"Don't worry about that now. Why don't you go take a shower and put on one of my nightgowns? By then the pizza will be here, and we can watch a movie on cable."

Renee pulled herself up from the couch and trudged up the stairs. Her tired, defeated walk reminded me of myself after Sam died. A simple thing like taking a shower took a supreme effort.

I knew how Renee felt. I, too, had been abandoned. Except Sam had died instead of finding someone else. Death, the ultimate betrayal. Absolutely no way to undo the end.

The picture of me cradling Sam in my arms is as clear now as it was the night it happened. Mom says I'll never forget that. Renee stuck with me through those first awful months. I was determined to stick with her now when she was hurting so much.

Renee came down the stairs wearing my blue cotton nightgown. It dragged on the rug because she was so much shorter than I, but she looked refreshed and calmer.

"Lie down here." I motioned toward the couch. "I'll get the Cokes."

When I came back from the kitchen, Renee was combing her wet hair.

"Do you feel any better?"

"Yeah, a little. I sure am glad you were home."

"And where else would I be?"

"On Saturday night? I could think of a lot of places."

"I'm sure you could, but I'm happy right here. Work today was a killer."

"You going to keep working all those hours now that school has started?"

"Yeah, if I can. I need to save money for college next year. Tom pays at least half of his tuition and most of his expenses. I want to do the same thing."

"Still trying to compete with the perfect brother, huh?"

"No, not compete. I just want to help out all I can. Tom was considering taking a year off because there wasn't enough money for both of us to go to school. But we all talked it over and decided that if we pull together we can do it. Mom is due for a raise at the law office, and if Tom and I both take out student loans and work part-time we can swing it."

"Your family really sticks together. I envy you that."

"Not all the time." Tonight I didn't want to think about family squabbles. We'd had plenty of them when I was dating Sam.

When the pizza arrived, we were both ready to eat. "Sometimes food is the only way to cope with heartbreak," I assured Renee as we dug our fingers through the thick cheese. "Now if we can only find something chocolate for dessert, we'll be all set."

After we ate, we pulled out the hideabed and curled up to watch TV. We were both asleep when the phone rang about midnight.

"Hello," I mumbled into the receiver.

"Is Renee there?"

Instantly I recognized Renee's mother's voice. I poked Renee to wake her up. "It's your mom," I whispered to her, holding my hand over the mouthpiece. "She wants to know if you're here."

Renee sighed, as she took the receiver from me. "Yeah, Mom, I'm here. Yes, we got into a fight and I came home. I stopped to see Jeannie and I guess I fell asleep. Yes, I was planning on coming home. I just wanted to talk to Jeannie for a while. Why can't I just stay here now, since it's so late? Please."

For ten minutes Renee begged. Finally her mother relented and Renee promised she'd be home first thing in the morning.

"Do you believe that jerk? He called my house a few minutes ago, looking for me. Gave my mother some stupid sob story about how we got into a little spat and I took off. He said I never told him I was leaving and he's so worried."

21

"Right. Did he by any chance mention what your 'little spat' was about?"

"Of course not. My dear, gullible mother, who believes anything he says, is mad at me for taking off without telling him. And even madder because I didn't come home."

"Will you tell her what really happened?"

"I suppose. She'll find out anyway from someone else, so I might as well tell her myself. But somehow I know she'll decide this is all my fault. You know how she thinks men are superior beings and it's the duty of every woman to spend her life making a man happy."

"She's not the only woman who thinks like that." I knew lots of people who thought the same way.

"Geez, sometimes the way she gives in to my dad makes me sick."

I smiled, remembering all the times I saw Renee doing the same thing with Brian. Maybe there was hope for her after all.

"And don't you say a word. I know what you're thinking." Renee and I had argued more than once about how men and women should treat each other.

"I won't. Not tonight anyway."

"Good. Now I'm going back to sleep."

I flipped the lamp switch and waited for sleep to come again.

Chapter 3

Tuesday morning Renee managed to hide the dark circles under her eyes with makeup, but I could still see them.

"How are you feeling?" I studied her face as she drove.

"A little better. I'm glad we have school. It beats sitting home feeling sorry for myself." I admired Renee's efforts to keep herself going in spite of how depressed she was.

"That's true. Did you hear from Brian?"

"Not a word. I think I told you Mom called him back Saturday night to tell him I was at your house and I was all right. The jerk hasn't bothered to call since."

"Do you think he will?"

"If he had any guts at all, he'd at least call and explain himself. Last night I had to practically tie my hands to my bed to keep from dialing his number. But I'm determined. If he doesn't call me, I'm not going to call him and make a fool of myself again."

"Maybe he doesn't know what to say."

"He knew what to say Saturday night to my mother. Got me in a ton of trouble."

"Maybe he really was worried about you."

"Ha! Feeling guilty about behaving like such slime is more like it."

"How's your mom? Yesterday you said she was calming down a little."

"She is. She's still mad at me for not coming home or calling her, but she'll get over it. And just like I predicted, she thinks this is all my fault."

"How about your dad?"

"Who knows? He's probably glad Brian dumped me."

"Brian didn't dump you. Don't do that to yourself."

"What do you call it, then?"

"A temporary lapse of sanity. I think he'll come around."

"If he does he'll probably have the blonde bombshell on his arm."

A car honked as it sped by us.

"That crazy Rich. One of these days he's going to dent that souped-up car of his and then he'll be sorry." Renee stepped on the accelerator, swung around Rich, and cut him off at the entrance to the school parking lot.

"Hey, take it easy, will you? I'd like to complete senior year with my body intact if you don't mind." I hated it when Renee drove recklessly.

Renee laughed. "Sorry."

"At least you're smiling," I said to her.

"The first time in three days. Oh, look. Trent is with Rich again. You know, Jeannie, I've been thinking. If Brian has a new girlfriend, there's no reason why I should just sit around and wait for him, is there?"

"Of course not." I knew what was coming. And I hoped I was wrong.

"And perhaps one of those gentlemen in that car is a possibility."

"Rich is a real nice guy. He likes to have fun and party just like you do." I knew it wasn't Rich she was interested in, but I wanted to postpone hearing the truth.

"Rich? Who cares about Rich? It's the cowboy I'm talking about."

"Oh." I swallowed hard. For the first time since Sam, I felt a genuine interest in a guy. Why did Renee have to notice him too? "Gee, I didn't think cowboy boots were your style." I felt sick to my stomach. I realized I'd been thinking about Trent on and off all weekend. I hadn't thought about a guy that much since Sam.

"Maybe they're not his, either."

"I don't know. I kind of like them on him."

Renee turned and stared at me, but I looked away. Had I given myself away? In spite of the boots I suspected Trent was more Renee's type than mine. I tried to push away the feeling of envy I was experiencing.

"Hi, guys," Renee yelled out the window to Rich and Trent.

"That little Mustang of yours isn't going to look so pretty if you cut off the wrong person," Rich said.

"I was just saying the same thing to Jeannie about your car."

"Want to drag?" Rich asked.

"I wouldn't want to embarrass you, Rich. Me being a girl and all. I'd leave you in my dust."

"Now that is downright humorous. What do you say? On the Boulevard tonight?"

"I'll think about it."

"Don't be stupid, Renee." I couldn't believe she

was considering racing her new car down the very street where Sam got killed.

Renee pulled away. "Relax, will you? I'm only playing. Trent doesn't have much to say, does he?"

I didn't answer. I thought he had a lot to say last week.

"I think I'll like the strong, silent type for a change."

"You're serious about hustling this guy, aren't you?"

"Maybe. Besides, think how jealous Brian would be if I'm dating the new football star. You heard Rich say Trent is great."

"I doubt he's better than Brian."

"At this moment I hope he's ten times better. I hope he breaks every record this school has. And I hope he does it on Homecoming Weekend, too."

"Why?"

"Because Brian will be here, and I'd like to see him jealous."

"Brian's coming for Homecoming? Doesn't he have games on weekends?"

"Yeah, but that weekend they play on Friday. So he's planning to come home after practice on Saturday. You don't think he'd miss getting all that attention, do you? Returning hero and all."

"And you're thinking he'd be jealous seeing you with Trent, right?"

"It's an idea. I thought maybe I could play at his game as well as he does."

"What about Trent? Maybe he won't want to play."

"What do you mean? Don't you think Trent would want to go out with me?"

"I didn't say that."

"What's the matter, then?"

"Nothing. I just hate to see you using him to get back at Brian."

"I don't intend to use him. I'm just talking about a date. Besides, he's new here. I can introduce him around, make him feel part of the school. That's not using him, is it?"

"No, I guess not."

"What's wrong, then? I can tell something's bothering you. Do you think I should sit around and wait for Brian, is that it?"

"No, I didn't say that. I just think maybe you should give yourself a little time before you get all involved with another guy."

"I'm not getting involved. I'm just talking about a date or two."

Somehow I didn't trust that. Because Trent was new here, he would probably be delighted to go out with someone as popular as Renee. The truth was that I was jealous and didn't know what to do.

"You know what your problem is, Jeannie?"

"What?"

"You need a boyfriend. This celibate life you lead has got to stop. Maybe if I go out with Trent, we could double with you and Tim Murphy. You know he's dying to go out with you again."

"Thanks, but I can take care of my social life myself." I'd had a good enough time with Tim, but I knew I wasn't about to fall in love with him.

"Then get to it, girl. Homecoming is only a month away."

I shook my head as I got out of the car. This was one time I couldn't tell Renee what I was really feeling. I wanted to go to Homecoming with Trent, not Tim Murphy.

On my way into the building I spotted Trent leaning against a locker talking to Rich. Was Renee his
type? Maybe he wouldn't want to go out with her.
Then I felt guilty. Renee had just been jilted by
Brian, yet she was determined not to let it get to her.
I ought to be happy she was doing something for
herself. She deserved someone who not only had
looks, but was sensitive and caring, too. I'd talked to
Trent only that one time, but somehow I knew that's
how he was. I should be happy Renee was interested
in a guy like Trent.

When I glanced Trent's way again, he was looking
right at me. He smiled. I was so surprised and embarrassed I turned away without acknowledging him.
When I looked again, his back was to me.

I wanted to kick myself for not smiling at him.
And then to add to my frustration, Renee chose that
moment to stop and chat with him and Rich. Her
plan was already in motion. I wondered how quickly
word would spread that she and Brian had broken up.
Knowing the speed of the school gossip vine, about
ten minutes.

My first-hour class was community and social is-
sues. Jeb was in the same class. On the first day we
claimed seats together in the back row. Jeb's com-
mentary about our fellow students and life in general
often made me laugh. It was easy to see why he and
Sam had been good friends. Both had pretty pessi-
mistic views of people. I figured it was because they
didn't have a lot in life to be optimistic about. Jeb's
dad used to work at the same factory my dad did, but
he wasn't working there any more. Dad told me he'd
quit after getting into trouble one night. Jeb's parents
drank a lot, too. It didn't sound like he had much of
a family life.

One day last spring Jeb had confided in me that he and his dad fought a lot, and not just with words. A couple of times after that when I saw bruises on his face or arms I figured he and his dad had been at it again. I tried to talk about it, but he just shrugged it off. When Jeb was ready he'd tell me what he wanted me to know.

I tried to concentrate while Mrs. Schoem discussed why it was important to be a smart consumer. I already knew a lot of what she was saying. My mom knew a good bargain and taught me early to save where and when I could. In sixth grade I'd opened a savings account and this summer I opened my own checking account. Mom was determined I'd know how to handle money before I left home. She didn't want me to blow my entire savings my first month in college.

When Mrs. Schoem started talking about our class projects, I forced myself to listen.

"As I mentioned earlier, each of you is required to do a class project. It can be service-oriented or deal with health awareness, public information, or business. The possibilities are unlimited. So in the next couple of weeks you need to brainstorm to come up with the right idea."

"Can we work with a partner or on a team?" Jeb asked.

"Under certain circumstances I'd allow that."

"What circumstances?"

"The main one is that everybody does his or her share of the work."

"You mean I can't get Jeannie as my partner and then let her do the work?"

"No, Jeb, you can't. But it's a good try."

"Just kidding, Mrs. Schoem. Knowing Jeannie, I'd be the one doing all the work."

The class laughed. I looked at Jeb and shook my head. It was good to hear him laughing. From the look of his face he'd had another fight over the weekend. I hadn't seen him smile all morning.

"This is like a report, huh?" a kid in the front row asked.

"I want more than just a report of facts. For example, right now professional athletes involved with drugs is a real problem. Interviews and suggestions on how to deal with the problem of drugs and alcohol with our school athletes would be a possibility."

"You think kids are going to talk?"

"Not for me they aren't. But I bet they would to you if they are guaranteed confidentiality."

"Meaning we wouldn't squeal."

"Exactly. Two years ago someone in this class did a fantastic investigation on some of the real horrors of freshman initiation. That was all done anonymously. It was published in the school paper."

"I remember that. I think it helped, too. A lot of the real mean stuff was stopped after that," one of the girls said.

"Are you kidding? It still goes on," a guy added.

"Do you think it's as bad as it once was?" Mrs. Schoem asked.

"Maybe not as bad," the guy conceded.

"Then maybe we did some good. A change has to start somewhere, even if it's a minor one."

I liked Mrs. Schoem's philosophy. For once the work had real meaning. That is, if I picked a good topic. I'd have to think about it for a while.

"Can we work with kids in your other sections?" She taught three of them.

"That doesn't work very well because I often give you class time to work, but I won't absolutely rule it out. Come up with a project and an idea and we can talk about it."

I liked the way she left things open. I liked her for respecting us.

Chapter 4

After class Jeb walked down the hall with me.

"How's everything at home?" I asked him.

"Don't ask."

"Bad, huh?"

"*Bad* I could handle. Out of control is more like it."

"What's going on?"

"It's my old man. He's been driving us crazy since he got laid off in June."

"Not working must be rough on him." I thought Dad had said Jeb's father quit. Maybe I'd misunderstood him.

"It's rougher on us. He fights with Ma all day, then I come home and he starts on me."

"Is he drinking?"

Jeb shrugged his shoulders. He hated it whenever I mentioned that subject.

"Jeb, I hear the new school social worker is a real good guy. Why don't you talk to him?"

"Jeannie, lay off that social worker crap, will you. I'm not going to talk about my problems at home to some jerk adult I don't even know."

"Maybe he's not a jerk. And besides, once you start talking to him you'll get to know him. Trust me,

Jeb, I know it would help if you had somebody to talk to.''

"No, it won't. And don't give me your speech about how terrific a social worker can be. I don't want to hear it.''

Jeb stomped off and I stood in the hall feeling awful. Why couldn't I learn to keep my mouth shut? Just because talking with a social worker had helped me after Sam died, that didn't mean it would work for everybody. But it sure seemed to me Jeb needed someone to listen to him. I hoped he had a friend he could talk to, but I didn't really think he did.

"Hey, Jeannie, wait up.'' Rich waved to me from the end of the corridor. I waited.

"Is it true Renee broke up with Brian?''

I smiled. It had taken all of an hour. "Yes, Rich, it is.''

"I can't believe it. I thought those two would be hitting the aisle for sure in a few years.''

I felt like saying "So did Renee,'' but I didn't. "It happens.''

"I guess it does. Well, I got to run. Hey, talk her into bringing that new blue Mustang to the Boulevard tonight, will you?''

"No way, Rich. You're talking to the wrong person here. I intend to do my best to keep her away from there.''

"Why? Nobody's going to play chicken. Just some little wheelie-dealie.''

"Your wheelie-dealie is for kids on dirt bikes, not in cars. Oh, Rich, for such a smart guy sometimes you act like a jerk.''

"What can I say?''

"Nothing, believe me. Not a thing.''

"But I'm cute, right?''

"Fair, pal, fair." I wanted to ask him where Trent was, but I stopped myself, Renee had already staked out that territory, and a best friend would not interfere.

That night Dad was late for supper. When he didn't walk in the door at 5:30 or phone, Mom and I both suspected trouble. Mom had cooked spaghetti and I had tossed a salad. The garlic bread was drying out in the oven. Finally, at 6:30, we heard a car in the driveway.

One look at his face and we both knew he'd had a hard day.

"Hi, honey. How about something cold to drink?" Mom pulled a Coke from the refrigerator and handed it to him.

"Thanks." He popped the top, took a long swallow, and picked up the newspaper.

Mom let him rest and read the sports section for a few minutes before she set the spaghetti on the table.

When I pulled the bread from the oven, Dad laid the paper aside and reached for the salad. "Had a real mess today when the shift changed." Since Dad was the day foreman, he was responsible for any trouble.

"What happened?" Mom asked.

"Earl Mitchell showed up and demanded to be put back on the line." Earl Mitchell was Jeb's father.

"I thought he quit," Mom said.

"He did. But now he's claiming he was forced to quit and is demanding his job back." I had heard Dad right. Jeb's dad hadn't been laid off at all.

"Can he do that?" Mom asked.

"No, but he did manage to cause a lot of trouble. When Mitchell came in, he was three sheets to the wind and looking for a fight. He got one, too. The security guard finally had to belt him with his billy club. He was bleeding pretty bad. When the ambulance got there, the attendant said he'd need stitches.''

''Doesn't sound like that family is doing so well,'' Mom said.

''They're not,'' I told them. ''Jeb comes to school some days looking like he hasn't slept at all.''

''And now his Dad's in the hospital. Do you suppose they have insurance?'' Mom asked.

''No way. His insurance ran out thirty days after he walked out of the factory. And you can bet they didn't have money to pay it on their own.''

''Do you see Jeb much?'' Mom asked me.

''I didn't over the summer, but now I do. He's in my first-period class. Just this morning he told me how bad things were at home. This will only make them worse.''

''Life sure is hard for some people,'' Mom said. Working at the law office had been a real eye opener for Mom. She couldn't believe how nasty some people could be or how bad off others were emotionally. Soft-hearted Mom had a hard time accepting human miseries. I liked that about her.

''One of these days that guy is going to drink himself into the grave.'' Dad dug his fork into the salad before turning to Mom again. ''How are things at your office, Margaret?''

''Hectic. Once summer's over the work pours in. But I like being busy.''

''Did we get a letter from Tom?'' Dad asked.

''No. If we don't hear from him by the end of the week, let's call him Saturday.''

''What makes you think he'll be around? Rumor has it he and Cynthia are keeping pretty steady company these days,'' I said.

''I suspect you're right. I just hope he gets law

35

school under his belt before he thinks about getting married,'' Mom said.

"But, honey, we didn't wait. Why should they?" Dad asked.

"Because this is a new generation, and they're supposed to be smarter than we were," Mom answered.

"Falling in love doesn't have anything to do with IQ.''

"I know," Mom said with a sigh.

It was nice to think about Tom being in love. He had always been such a hard worker he hadn't dated a lot in high school. Renee calls Tom "Mr. Perfect." She is right in a way, too. Sometimes teachers who knew Tom expect me to be like him. That used to bother me, but not any more. Somehow I've managed to make my own way and I'm glad.

Now he had Cynthia. She was pretty and smart and liked Tom a lot. It was fun to see Tom so happy. Secretly I thought maybe she wasn't good enough for him, but then I decided nobody was going to be good enough for my brother. I wondered if he thought the same about me. He sure hadn't thought Sam was right for me.

From the very beginning Tom had been vehement that I stay away from Sam. But eventually Tom came around. At the end he'd even apologized and told me how sorry he was he hadn't given Sam more of a chance. I liked him a lot for that. He wasn't afraid to admit when he was wrong.

For some reason I thought of Trent. I wondered if he could easily admit being wrong. After school today I'd seen him near the football locker room. His cowboy boots clicked as he walked. He looked so good in his Levi's. Something about the way he walked reminded me of Sam. Maybe it was the confidence. That alone should have been enough to scare me off.

I was clearing the table when the phone rang. It was Renee.

"Want to go to Arly's for a while? See what's happening?"

"Not if you're going to play wheelie-dealie with Rich."

"Oh, Rich was just talking. I'm not going to play that stupid game. Come with me. Just for half an hour."

"You promise me you're not going to do anything crazy with your car?"

"Jeannie, I love this car. Do you really think I'd do anything wild with it?"

"Yes, I do."

She laughed. "I'll pick you up in half an hour."

As soon as I hung up, I regretted saying yes. I had a ton of homework and whenever Renee said half an hour, it meant an hour. And deep down I knew why I was going. I wanted to see Trent. In spite of telling myself he was for Renee, I didn't believe it. I had to see if my attraction for him was real.

Arly's was jammed. It amazed me that no one was home studying. It looked like a Friday night. I wondered if any one besides me was worried about getting into college or getting a scholarship. But then I had to laugh. Here I was, out cruising on a school night just like the rest of them.

Renee spotted Rich's car and pulled up right beside it. Rich and Trent were leaning against the trunk.

"Sorry to hear about you and Brian," Rich said.

"What's to be sorry about? I'm not." Renee tried to sound unaffected by it all.

"Well, that's good. I'm surprised though. You two were always together," Rich said.

"Breaking up seemed like the sensible thing to do with him away at college and me here. A girl has to have a little fun, especially senior year, don't you think?" She looked at Trent and flashed him her finest smile.

Trent drank it all in and a slow grin crept across his face. Then he shrugged his shoulders and nodded yes.

"You have the cutest dimples. I suppose everybody tells you that." Renee reached up and poked her finger in Trent's left dimple. I was sure he'd pull away, but he didn't flinch. So he likes the flirty type. That eliminates me, I decided.

"So, Cowboy, tell us all about yourself. How did we get so lucky?" Renee jumped onto the hood of Rich's car. I stood there, not sure what to do.

Trent shrugged his shoulders a second time. But that didn't stop Renee.

"Does everyone in the city wear those?" Renee pointed toward the boots.

"A few do."

He seemed much quieter and more reserved tonight than he had in the courtyard. I wondered why.

"Do you ride horses?" Renee asked.

"Sometimes."

"Sheila Anderson said you're living right down the street from her with your grandparents."

Sheila's family was loaded and lived in the rich section of town.

"What else did she say?" Trent's smile became a frown. He stood up straight and stepped toward Renee.

"That's all. Is it a secret or something, where

38

you're living?" Renee tried to shrug off his sudden seriousness.

"No, of course not. Sorry." He backed up and leaned against the fender.

For a few seconds nobody said anything. Renee looked at me. I didn't know what to say. Neither one of us had a clue to what had upset Trent.

"This must be a real switch from the big-time city," Renee said, trying to clear the tension from the air.

"A little," he answered. Renee had apparently pumped Sheila for information. What else did Renee know about Trent?

While Renee and Trent talked, I studied Trent's fine chiseled face. He was tan and clean shaven. His black hair was styled and neatly combed. I could see why Renee and probably tons of other girls would think he was pretty special. But I sensed there was more to Trent than his good looks. Behind those blue eyes loomed a lifetime of stories. I wanted to know what they were.

"And you're a football player, too. Lincoln High sure got lucky when you came to town." I watched Renee, trying to determine if her compliments were genuine. I sensed they were. Her smile was real and I knew for the moment the pain Brian caused her was forgotten.

"Do you like football?" he asked Renee.

"I sure do. Especially the players who are so strong." She reached over and touched his bicep. I wanted to grab her hands and tell her to keep them to herself. I wanted Trent to tell her that.

"What about you?"

It took me a second to realize Trent was talking to me. I wasn't sure what he'd asked. "Pardon me?" I mumbled.

"Football. You like it?"

Renee laughed out loud. "Oh, Trent, you don't know how funny that is. Jeannie barely knows what a football is. Jocks have never been her type. Right?" Renee waited for me to answer. I couldn't think of what to say.

Finally Renee came to my rescue. "Now I'm another story. I just love football." Out of the corner of her eye Renee watched me. My silence had confused her.

Trent looked back at Renee. I sensed something behind those blue eyes, but I couldn't tell what it was. At that moment I wished I could be as flirtatious and talkative as Renee.

When Rich started discussing next week's game. I snuck inside Arly's for a Coke. I felt like a jerk for not answering Trent. But what difference did it make? Trent was a jock and Renee was right. Jocks weren't my type. But what was my type? After Sam, nobody seemed right for me. Until Trent.

Chapter 5

Renee and Trent seemed to become a couple during the next three weeks. I could hardly stand to see them together, and it was torture listening to Renee talk about how sweet Trent was. The morning ride to school became unbearable. Finally I couldn't take it anymore and told Renee I was going to walk to school. Needed the exercise, I said. That worked for a few days, but one Friday morning Renee came to my house early and insisted I ride to school with her.

When I got in the car she didn't waste any time. "Okay, friend, what's going on? I know the cold-shoulder treatment when I get it." Renee crinkled her forehead and gave me one of her long "I know you" looks.

"What are you talking about?" I wished I'd never gotten into her car.

"I'm talking about why you've been avoiding me lately. Do I have bad breath or something?"

"Of course not."

"Then what is it? When I first broke up with Brian you stuck with me like glue, but this last couple of weeks I've hardly seen you. What gives?"

"I'm surprised you noticed." The sarcasm was

heavier than I'd intended and I regretted the remark. Why did I have to start a fight?

"Now what does that mean?"

"Nothing." Maybe I could still avoid an argument.

"No. Nothing doesn't work. Does this have to do with Trent?"

"What makes you think that?"

"I just think it does."

I didn't answer. Let her think what she wanted to. I wasn't about to tell her what really upset me.

"I know you don't like him, but does that mean you have to avoid me and be rude to him?"

I couldn't believe she thought I didn't like him, but I was relieved. It was easier to let her believe that than to tell her the truth. But I hated the idea that I'd been rude to Trent.

"What do you mean?" I asked.

"It's obvious. You barely speak to him."

"He barely speaks to me. But I've never been rude to him. I don't know why you'd say that."

"Maybe not rude, but distant. Trent thinks you don't like him."

"Trent thinks that?" I wanted to cry.

"He told me he met you the first day of school out in the Circle when that idiot fired that starter gun. He said you both got caught in the mob scene. You talked that day, but since then you've hardly spoken to him."

"That's not true. I speak to him. His problem is that he's so infatuated with you he doesn't know anyone else is around."

"I doubt it," Renee protested, but I could tell she liked what I said. "I told him you were shy, but he said you didn't seem shy in the courtyard. How come

42

you didn't tell me about meeting him that day, anyway?"

"Because it was so humiliating. Here I was, sprawled out like a fool, and I couldn't get up. Then this guy I don't even know comes along and helps me. I was so embarrassed that I just wanted to forget it ever happened. I'm sure he was laughing when he told you about how we met."

"No, not at all. He never even mentioned that part. He did say he's tried talking to you a couple of times since then and you ignored him. I'm telling you, he thinks you don't like him."

"Well, he's wrong."

"You do like him, then?"

"I barely know him, Renee. From what I do know though, he seems all right." All right was an understatement. But I couldn't admit that to Renee.

"Well, if you talked to him you'd get to know him."

Renee didn't know what she was saying. I wanted nothing more than to get to know him. I spent half my waking hours thinking of Trent. "Believe me, Renee, I like him just fine. Really I do."

"I thought maybe you were jealous."

"Me jealous? Don't be ridiculous." I could feel my face turning red.

"I just thought maybe you didn't like it I found somebody so soon after Brian. Here it's been three years since Sam, and you still don't have anyone."

"I've had offers, Renee. I'm just not interested. The guys I've dated were either total bores or total animals. I want something else."

"Like what?"

"Like somebody I can talk to, laugh with, share secrets with. You know what I mean."

43

"Sure, but maybe you're being too fussy. How about going to the Homecoming dance? You could double with Trent and me."

"Trent already asked you?"

"Yes, last weekend. It's going to feel real strange going to a school dance with Trent and not Brian. But I have to admit I'm looking forward to the look on Brian's face when he sees me with Trent. Do you think it's weird that I want to get even?"

"No. But I still hate the idea of you using Trent."

"Oh, it's not like that at all. Trent is really a great guy. He's so sensitive. Actually, he's a lot like you. I told him that, too. Just last night I told him he really would like talking with you. I wish you'd give him a chance. He's not like Brian at all. Believe me."

"I know he's not." It was almost funny, the way Renee was defending Trent to me. Except it hurt too much to be funny.

"So will you give him a chance? Want to go to Homecoming with us?"

"Three might be kind of a crowd."

"Oh, I didn't mean just you by yourself. Tim's dying to ask you. He's a real sweetheart. We'll have a great time."

"Yeah, Tim's all right, but I don't know."

"Why not? Are you going to sit home all senior year? That's dumb."

"Maybe I'll go. Let me think about it for a while. Are you sure Tim wants to go with me?"

"Yeah, he told me. He said he had a great time when we all went to the movies. Remember?"

"Yes, that was fun. But it bothered me that he kept asking questions about Sam. I didn't like that."

44

"Well, did you tell him you didn't want to talk about Sam?"

"Yeah. And then I felt like a fool. Oh, Renee, I don't know."

"Please. It'll be a lot of fun."

"I'll think about it."

"Well, think yes. Oops, here we are. I have to run. See you after school."

I wasn't exactly thrilled about going to the dance with Tim. But I didn't really want to stay home, either. And I had promised myself this year was going to be different. Besides, I liked to dance and I remembered Tim was a good dancer. That could be fun if there was a good band.

Mom and Dad went dancing a lot. When I was little, Dad taught me different dance steps. I had great rhythm, Dad said. When Tom was learning to dance, I was his partner. We'd spent many an afternoon trying to get Tom's two left feet to move to the music. For someone so smart, he sure was clumsy.

I had never danced with Sam. To this day I wished we could have danced together just once. I wondered if Trent could dance. Somehow, I could envision those cowboy boots gliding across the floor.

Jeb was slumped in his seat when I got to class. He didn't even look up when I dropped my books on the floor.

"Morning," I said, poking him in the ribs.

He scowled.

"What's wrong?" I asked.

When he looked up, I saw his black eye.

"Fight with your dad?"

He nodded. "But this is the last time. I told him that, too."

I felt sick to my stomach. "You did?"

"Yup. I told him if he ever hits me again, that's it. And I mean it, too. The next time he comes at me, he's had it."

"How are things now?" The thought of Tom or me physically fighting with Dad or Mom was too awful to imagine. And Jeb had to live with that threat daily.

"Oh, just fine. He kicked me out."

"Of your house?"

"Yup. He told me he was the boss there and he'd do whatever he wanted, and if I didn't like it I could find someplace else to live. I was so angry that I ran out of the house. When I came back a couple of hours later, my things were dumped all over the front yard."

"Oh, Jeb."

"I slept in our garage last night. I didn't know what else to do." Tears filled his eyes. He looked away.

"Hey, it's all right." I touched him on the arm. "We'll figure out something."

I wanted to cry for him. Ever since I'd come to know Jeb freshman year I had liked him. Oh, not at first. His sarcastic remarks and long hair bothered me, but then I discovered there was so much more under that rough exterior. All through class I tried to figure out some way to help Jeb.

After class I walked down the hall with him.

"What about going home after school and trying to talk to your dad? Maybe he'll let you come home."

"I suppose I'll have to. I don't know what else to do."

"What about your mom?"

"What about her? She's useless. She does what

ever he says. If only he'd get called back to the factory. Then things would be better.''

''I don't think that's going to happen.'' Jeb was dreaming if he thought that was possible.

''Why not? Other times he's gotten called back.''

''Yeah, but that's because before he was laid off. This is different.''

''What do you mean this is different? Laid off is laid off.''

I looked hard at Jeb, trying to figure out if he really believed his dad had been laid off or if he knew the truth and was just denying it. Finally I said, ''Your dad quit, Jeb. He didn't get laid off.''

''What are you talking about? The whole crew got let go.''

I must have had a strange look on my face. Was I a fool for blabbing the truth? I didn't know how to answer Jeb. I looked away.

''Do you know something I don't?'' He grabbed my arm to get my attention.

''I could have gotten it wrong, Jeb. You better ask your dad.''

''Got what wrong?''

''About him not getting laid off.'' I didn't know what else to say. I regretted I'd ever started this. But some part of me knew Jeb deserved to know the truth.

''Jeannie, tell me what you're talking about.''

I hesitated. ''I could be wrong, Jeb, but I heard your dad came in one night pretty drunk, got in an argument with the night foreman, and stomped off in a huff. He came back a little while later and announced he quit.''

''You heard it wrong. He got laid off. He said he did.''

"Jeb, you know my dad's the day foreman. He's the one who told me that."

"Well, I don't believe it. Dad's going to get called back. I just know it. Then things will be better. You just wait and see."

My heart ached for Jeb. He was living in a fantasy world. He refused to see his father for what he was. Maybe it was the only way for him to survive. What would Jeb do if he couldn't go back home? If Sam were still alive, Jeb could have stayed at his house, but now he was on his own. I watched him walk away. I called to him, but he didn't look back.

Chapter 6

During Homecoming Week the student council planned daily activities to boost school spirit—Dress Up Day, Turnabout Day, a pep rally, and the bonfire on Friday night. I'd agreed to go to the dance with Tim, but I couldn't really get into the spirit of things.

Tim was very attentive, but I found myself avoiding him at times. Every time he mentioned the dance, I dreaded the idea of being so close to Trent for an entire evening and yet so distant.

Friday night was a clear, unseasonably warm October evening. A perfect night for the bonfire. Renee called about seven o'clock. She and Trent offered to pick me up. I told her thanks, but no, I'd meet them there. A whole night with Trent and Renee was going to be hard enough. I didn't need to torture myself more.

The feel in the air reminded me of the first evening I'd spent with Sam. I smiled thinking of it. A date with Tim was so different from the dates I had with Sam. Sam didn't go for school functions. I could almost hear him laughing about them. But Sam had been a long time ago. Three years seemed like an eternity, yet Sam was still very real to me. I could picture him as clear as day. Those beautiful brown eyes, that lazy grin, the dimple in his chin. Even thinking about him sent chills through my body. I'd kissed a few guys since Sam, but none of them compared to Sam. Sometimes I was sure I'd never again feel what I felt with Sam. Thoughts of Trent entered my head, but I pushed them aside.

At the bonfire, the flames crackled and leaped into the air. The football squad piled on wood and twigs to keep the fire blazing. Tim and Trent stood near the wood pile with the rest of the squad. Renee was with the pom-pom squad. Cheer after cheer echoed across the field.

The football coach used a bullhorn to get everyone's attention. I wandered over to a group of kids I knew. Gradually the cheering and noise subsided.

The coach attempted a rousing speech. Most everybody ignored him. But when he introduced the football team, he got everyone's attention. Football players were major heroes, especially if they were winning, and so far they had lost only one game.

The girls near me had a comment for every guy. I didn't say much, but I laughed as they passed judgment on every player. Sheila was the most astute observer.

"Get a load of that gorgeous hunk of man." She pointed toward the co-captain.

"Forget it, Sheila, he's taken," Laura warned her.

"I know, but looking's free, isn't it?"

We all laughed. Sheila wasn't afraid to say what she thought.

"Now what about that one?" The coach introduced Trent. The crowd cheered. "Sure didn't take Renee long to snag him, did it?" Sheila said.

"About four seconds after Brian dumped her," Laura laughed.

"I can't say I blame her, though. He is gorgeous," Sheila said.

"He's so quiet though. You ever talk to him, Jeannie?" Laura asked me.

"Not much. We're doubling with them tomorrow night," I said.

"Yeah, I heard. You're going with Tim, right?" Sheila asked.

"Yes."

"Well, get all the info you can. Find out what he's really like. Find out if I should make my move," Sheila said.

"I'd like to see that," Laura laughed. "Seems to me he moved in on Renee real fast once he heard she was available. I doubt if he even knows the rest of us girls exist."

"You just love to dash my dreams, don't you?"

"Sorry. I'm just being realistic. Besides, what's he still doing here, anyway? I thought you told me they were moving back to the city," Laura asked.

"His mom did leave. But apparently he's going to stay here and live with his grandparents," Sheila said.

"Why?" Laura asked.

"I'm not sure." Something about the way Sheila answered made me wonder if she knew more than she was saying. But it wasn't like Sheila not to tell everything she knew.

"Does he have a father?" Laura asked.

"I guess so, but nobody's talking. His mom grew up here, but from what I hear she hasn't been back in years. Then one day she shows up with Trent and his sister."

I didn't know Trent had a sister. But then I didn't know anything about his family. Since Renee had been spending so much time with Trent, I'd bowed out. Now I wished I'd asked her more about him.

"His sister's gone, though. She went back with their mom," Sheila said.

"She did?"

"Yup. Trent is the only one still here."

"Sounds strange to me," Laura said. "Sheila, find out the scoop, will you?"

"I'll do my best," Sheila answered. And no doubt she would. Sheila was a great snoop.

I wondered what the story was with Trent's family. Maybe tomorrow night I'd find out myself from Trent.

"Whatever the story is, the guy is gorgeous. Even cuter than Brian. I have to hand it to Renee, she does know how to pick them," Laura said.

I had to agree, but why did she have to choose the one guy in three years I was interested in?

"I hear Brian is going to be at the dance tomorrow night. That ought to be real interesting." Sheila smiled.

I nodded yes. Tomorrow night had all the makings of a real melodrama. I hoped it would have a happy ending.

Renee was hyper after the pep rally. She bounced as she talked.

"I know we're going to win. I just feel it. And Brian will be in town, and I'll be with Trent. It's all so strange. Who would have believed this six weeks ago?"

"No one. You figure you being with Trent will even the score with Brian?"

"Nothing I could do to him would ever make up for the humiliation I felt that day at State. Besides, with my luck he won't even care."

"Come on. You and Brian meant a lot to each other. I can't imagine he'd forget you so quickly."

"But he did, didn't he?" Tears sprang to Renee's eyes.

"Hey, I'm sorry. I know this must still hurt."

"Oh, it's not your fault. I'm just glad I met Trent. I don't know what I'd do without him."

"He's going to be here the rest of the year too, from what Sheila just said."

"Yeah, his mom left last week, but he's staying here."

"Why'd she leave?"

"I'm not sure."

"Didn't you ask?"

"Sure, but Trent didn't seem to want to talk about it, so I didn't press it."

"Well, maybe you should. Maybe the guy needs someone to talk to."

"Hey, Jeannie, give me some credit. I may not know Trent real well, but I do respect his privacy. He knows that if he wants to talk I'll listen."

I didn't answer her right away. Why was I giving her a hard time? Of course Renee would listen. She'd listened to me plenty. I apologized to her.

"That's okay," she said. "Come on. Let's have some fun tonight. Want to check out Arly's?"

"No, thanks. I'm going home."

"Come on. I'm meeting Trent there, and I'm sure Tim'll be there."

"I know. I just don't feel like it. Okay?"

"Listen, you do what you want. I'm just glad you're doubling with us tomorrow. You're a real friend, Jeannie, you know that?"

"Thanks. So are you." I felt a stab of guilt. She wouldn't consider me such a great friend if she knew how much I liked Trent.

"Want me to pick you up for the parade?"

"No, thanks. I have to work in the morning. I'll see you at the game later."

On my way home I thought about Renee. Seeing Brian was going to be difficult for her, even with Trent. She and Brian had been together for three years. I really thought they loved each other, too. Brian's quick desertion seemed out of character. I wasn't surprised he wanted to date other girls, but I was surprised he totally abandoned Renee.

Brian and Renee seemed so right for each other. Oh, they'd had their share of fights, but they managed to get through them. I had always envied them that. I read somewhere the true measure of love is how well you can fight and endure. I liked that. I didn't think I'd be very good at it. Avoidance was what I preferred. Don't fight if you don't have to. A fight was too devastating for me. I was always too afraid of what I would lose. A part of me was lost every time I got into a fight. No matter who it was with.

On Saturday I worked until two. Mr. Nolan had agreed to give me the rest of the day off so I could go to the game and get ready for the dance. Even though I'm not a football fan, I'd promised Renee I'd be there to see the new routine the squad had been working on for weeks. Renee was to do a flip off the top of a human pyramid of eight girls. She was nervous, but she'd do fine. Renee loved being the star and was at her best in front of a crowd.

I got there just before halftime. Lincoln was winning. Trent was a key player, someone said.

The pom-pom squad was near the forty-yard line all decked out in new red skirts and white sweaters with white gloves and red top hats. Renee looked so

54

cute. The crowd loved the routine. They yelled and cheered and whistled. Renee's flip went perfectly and her face glowed when she marched off the field. I hurried over to the squad.

"You were terrific." I gave her a big hug.

"Thanks. I was so scared."

"Well, you couldn't tell. The crowd loved you."

She smiled and then leaned toward me. "Have you seen Brian?"

"No. Is he here?"

"I don't know. I just thought maybe he was. He always liked to watch me with the squad." She blushed.

"Yeah, I know he did." Brian loved to watch Renee perform. He'd always been so proud that Renee was on the squad. "I'll keep an eye out for him."

"Thanks, Jeannie. Our secret?"

"Our secret." I knew she didn't want anyone else to know how much she wanted to see Brian.

"I've got to run. See you later."

The squad left to change and I wandered back to the bleachers. Lincoln was winning, but the game bored me. Even watching Trent wasn't fun because the helmet blocked his face. I decided to leave so I'd have time to relax before the dance. I really wasn't looking forward to the evening. Just as I was leaving, there was a ruckus on the field. The referee called time out. Someone was down. It was Tim. The players hovered around him for a while, and then the coach helped him limp off the field. He couldn't step on his left foot.

"It looks like a sprained ankle," a spectator said.

Great, I thought. Now I won't even be able to dance tonight. Then I felt guilty. Here Tim was hurt and all I could think of was no dancing. I waited a few more minutes but couldn't see what was happening with Tim, so I went home.

About five o'clock Renee called.

"Where'd you go after halftime? I was looking all over for you. Did you know Tim got hurt?"

"Yeah, I was there. How is he?"

"He's all right. Bad sprain, but it's not broken."

"That's good."

"But the bad news is he can't have the Caddy tonight. And he's really upset. He's been dying to show off that car."

"It doesn't bother me." I meant it, too. But I suspected Renee was a little disappointed, especially since Trent didn't have a car. She'd been looking forward to being chauffeured in a Cadillac.

"So I guess we'll take my car. Trent can drive."

"Fine."

I smiled. Just like her to let Trent drive her car. She wouldn't want him to feel bad if she were driving.

Tim called a little while later.

"How's the foot?" One part of me hoped he had called to cancel our date. A night of sitting at a table making small talk sounded pretty grim at that moment.

"Not bad. Hurts a little, but I'll make it. But I won't be able to play for a couple of weeks at least. That's the worst part."

I hadn't even thought of that. I tried to be sympathetic, but I wasn't sure it came across that way.

"Listen, if you should stay off your foot, we don't have to go tonight." Here was his out.

"Oh, no. I told the doctor I had a date and that was all there was to it. He said no problem. As long as I stay off my ankle once we get there."

I considered telling him I didn't want to go, but I

knew I couldn't do that. Besides, I wanted to see Trent even if he was with Renee.

Mom came upstairs while I was getting ready.

"You look so pretty, Jeannie." She touched my dress, soft pink with ruffled sleeves and white lace trim.

"Thanks, Mom." I fastened a lace bow in my hair and turned to her.

"But you don't look happy. How come?"

I told her about Tim's foot. "That means I'm going to have to sit and talk to him all night. I don't know if I can. I don't know the slightest thing about football."

"Now, Jeannie, give the guy a chance. I'll bet he can talk about something other than sports."

I hoped she was right. Otherwise it was going to be a long night.

"Besides, I'm sure other boys will ask you to dance." Mom knew I loved to dance.

"I doubt it. The guys at Lincoln are so backward. They usually only dance with their dates."

"Well, you look beautiful tonight, and I want you to have a wonderful time."

"I'll try, Mom." But I knew it was going to be an effort.

When the door bell rang at 7:30, I answered it expecting to see Tim. Instead, Trent was standing on the front stairs. I gasped. He looked so gorgeous in a pinstriped navy suit with a light blue shirt and striped tie. I just stared. Finally my mom came to my rescue.

"Won't you come in?" she said, coming up behind me.

"Oh, yes." I finally tore my eyes from him. "Come in, Trent."

"I hope you don't mind that it's me. Tim can't walk too well, so I offered to pick you up."

"Of course not. Trent, this is my mom and dad."
I motioned to both of them. "Mom, Dad, this is
Trent Justin."

"Nice to meet you. Come and sit down if you
have time." Mom motioned to the living room.

"Thank you. We have a few minutes." Trent
followed me into the living room and sat down on the
couch.

"I know I'm early, but Renee wasn't ready so I
thought I'd pick up you and Tim and then go back
for her."

"Renee's never on time. You might as well get
used to it." I smiled. For once I was delighted at
Renee's slowness.

"I'm beginning to realize that." He smiled. I felt
my knees buckle. I jarred myself back to reality.
What was the matter with me? He was Renee's
boyfriend.

"You're new in town, right?" Mom asked.

"That's right," Trent answered.

"How do you like Lincoln High?" Mom asked.

"I like it fine."

"Is it similar to your old school?"

"Lincoln's smaller so it's much easier to find my
way around. And I've met more kids in six weeks
than I met the last three years. Of course, that's
pretty much due to Renee."

We all laughed.

"Yes, Renee does like to socialize," Mom said.

"Your parents move here?" Dad asked. I wanted
to die. I'd never mentioned Trent's home situation,
but then I didn't exactly know what it was.

"No, I'm living with my grandparents. My folks
are in the city."

"I see." I knew Dad didn't, but he tried to be

polite. He was trying so much harder than he ever had with Sam.

"And who are your grandparents? Might we know them?" Mom asked.

"Charlie and Evelyn Minion. They live on Oak Boulevard near 12th Street."

"Oh, sure. We know them. We went to school with their daughter Sally," Mom said.

"That's my mother."

"Well, I'll be." Dad said. He had a strange look on his face. Mom did, too.

"Sure, I remember her real well. That's where you get that handsome face. Your mom was a real beauty in high school," Mom said.

"She still is." Trent smiled and I knew he liked his mother a lot.

"Over the years I lost track of her. And now her son is sitting in our living room. Time sure does move on." Mom smiled at us both.

"Well, if you're ready, we should go. I told Tim I'd be there by eight," Trent said.

We walked to the front door. Trent opened it for me. "Nice meeting you," he said to my parents.

"Same here," Dad said.

"Have fun now and, Trent, make sure you dance with Jeannie tonight. She'll be real disappointed if she doesn't get to dance."

"Oh, Mom." I was mortified.

"I'll consider it my duty," Trent answered.

I just wanted to die. Why had Mom said that to him?

As soon as we were outside, I apologized. "I'm sorry. Don't pay any attention to her. And I hope their questions weren't too much. Sometimes my parents are so nosy."

"No problem. But isn't it weird that your parents knew my mom?"

"It sure is. Do you like living with your grandparents?"

"It's okay. I'd only seen them a couple of times my whole life and now I'm living with them. Strange."

I was dying to ask him more questions, but I didn't want to pry. Maybe later I'd have a chance to find out more about him.

"I bet it is."

"You like to dance?" Trent asked before I could find out more about his family.

"Sure, but ignore my mom. Sometimes she doesn't know when to be quiet."

"Why? I'd like to dance with you."

I wanted to scream, "And I'd like to dance with you," but I held myself back. What was I doing? Something told me to turn right around and run to my house. To fake sick or tired. Something else said don't be a fool. When Trent opened the car door, I stepped in. Whatever the night had in store, I wasn't going to miss it.

Chapter 7

The ride to Tim's house ended too quickly. When Tim came hobbling down the sidewalk as soon as we pulled up, I felt so disappointed. I wanted my time alone with Trent to last forever.

"Isn't this a bummer? My dad finally agrees to let me have the Caddy and this happens." Tim pointed to his taped ankle as he struggled to join me in the back seat.

"Don't worry about it. It doesn't matter. How's your ankle feel?" I was delighted he didn't have the Caddy. Trent picking me up instead of Tim and those few minutes alone with him made the whole evening worthwhile.

"Not too bad. I'm supposed to keep it elevated." He rested his heel on the back of the front seat and gently rubbed the elastic bandage.

"What did the doc say about you playing?" Trent turned to look at Tim. Our eyes met. I forced myself to look away.

"That's the worst part. He said I'd be out at least two weeks, maybe longer." Tim was too busy adjusting the bandage to notice my reaction to Trent.

The guys talked football the rest of the way to Renee's. I concentrated on the back of Trent's head.

Renee's mom insisted we all come in the house. Her dad pointed a videocamera at us as soon as we opened the front door. Tim limped around, made faces at the camera, and smiled a lot. I tried to stay out of camera range. Trent was camera shy, too. Renee and Tim made up for our lack of enthusiasm.

Renee served us soda in champagne glasses. Her dad proposed a toast to his lovely daughter and her friends. When we clicked our glasses my fingers accidently brushed Trent's. My whole body reacted to his touch. I could feel him all through me. My face turned red. I was afraid to look at him. Had he felt the same electricity?

We arrived at the dance a fashionable half-hour late. Renee wanted to make her grand entrance after everyone was there. It worked, too. The crowd paused when she came in on Trent's arm. I made an excuse to use the bathroom so I wouldn't have to follow them across the floor. I told Tim I'd meet him at our table.

A few minutes later when I joined them, Renee looked at me and gritted her teeth.

"What's wrong?" I asked her.

"He's here, all right. With her, too." Renee motioned across the room. Brian was standing near the punch table. A girl with long blonde hair had her arm linked through his.

"Forget about them and try to have a good time. Besides, she isn't half as pretty as you are. And Brian doesn't begin to compare to Trent."

"Are you kidding?" She looked at me like I was crazy. "You think Trent is better looking than Brian?" I guess love really is blind. There was no comparison, but obviously Renee's heart still belonged to Brian.

"They're both good-looking in their own way." I tried to be diplomatic.

"I didn't know you thought Trent was good-looking. You do, huh?"

I nodded yes. Good-looking was an understatement. I thought he was absolutely beautiful.

"Want to get something to drink?" Renee asked.

"I'm not thirsty. I don't think you are either." I knew she just wanted an excuse to walk past Brian.

"But I'm sure the fellows are. Shall we get some punch, guys?"

I tried to discourage her from going near Brian.

"Come with us, please," she begged me.

"Renee, you sure you want to do this?"

"I've got to get it over with sometime." She pushed her chair out and waited to take Trent's arm. They did make a beautiful couple crossing the dance floor.

"You go ahead. I'll stay here," Tim said.

"Okay," I said. I followed along feeling like a complete fool.

Brian turned as Renee and Trent approached the refreshment table.

He looked at her for a long time. It was the same loving look I'd seen so many times before. Freshman year that look used to make me gag, but I'd learned that I was just jealous. I was shocked his feelings were so apparent now. Suddenly I knew it wasn't over between Brian and Renee. My stomach did a flip-flop. If Renee and Brian got back together, Trent would be available. That idea was too exciting for me to contemplate.

Then Brian looked at Trent. His eyes clouded.

"Hi, Renee," Brian said. Immediately Sandy turned to look at us.

"Renee, you remember Sandy?" Brian said.

"Sure. This is Trent Justin. Trent, Brian and Sandy." She hugged his arm tight. "And my friend Jeannie Tanger," Renee motioned to me.

"Hi, Jeannie," Brian smiled at me. I had the strangest feeling he wanted to say something else, but didn't.

"Hello, Brian. Hi, Sandy," I said.

Trent stuck out his hand. For a second I thought Brian wasn't going to take it. But he did. Trent shook hands with Sandy, too.

"Such a darling little school you have here," Sandy said.

Darling, I thought. She sounds just like my cousin who thinks anything outside the big city is either darling, cute, or quaint.

"Darling?" Trent's eyebrows raised and he laughed.

"Yes, simply darling," she answered a little too quickly.

"What high school did you go to?" Trent asked her.

"Oh, a school in the city. I'm sure you wouldn't know it."

"I might. Which one?" Trent didn't let her off the hook. I liked it. Brian and Renee were too busy eyeing each other to be aware of the exchange. Finally Brian pulled himself back to the conversation.

"Sandy graduated from one of those fancy city schools. What was the name of it? I forgot."

"Yes, what was it?" Trent asked. Why was he being so persistent? He seemed determined not to let Sandy get away with her superior attitude. Was he already so attached to Renee he didn't want anyone insulting her? I was glad for her, but sad for me.

"Eastside High," she mumbled.

"Eastside. Oh, I know that school. Not as big as Lincoln. About 800 students, right? Public school like this too, isn't it?"

Trent had made his point. I loved him for it. He was helping Renee and I don't think she even realized it.

Sandy glared at Trent.

Trent smiled at her and turned to Brian. "Renee tells me you play football for State."

"I try."

"State's got a good team this year. You should do well."

"I hope so. Do you play football?"

"He sure does. He scored a touchdown today, didn't you, Trent?"

Trent shrugged his shoulders. Sandy was giving him an icy stare. I wanted to laugh out loud. Brian had missed the whole thing. He couldn't take his eyes off Renee. If Renee would loosen up a little and smile at him, I had the feeling Sandy wouldn't stand a chance.

"Brian, honey, would you get me some punch?" Sandy tried to get Brian to move. He looked at her, but he wasn't really seeing her. "I'll go with you." Sandy steered Brian away without another word to any of us. Renee's competition wasn't so tough after all.

When we got back to our table Renee tried to be cheerful. I knew she was depressed, though. Lots of kids were talking to Brian and eyeing Sandy. She *was* very pretty, but it was a porcelain beauty. It said look, but don't touch. Renee maybe wasn't as beautiful, but she was full of life and warmth. From the way Brian looked at Renee, it seemed like he was beginning to realize that.

To hide her feelings Renee decided to flit from table to table and group to group, talking and laughing. Trent followed her the first few moves, but then he gave up. I was glad when he came back and sat down beside me.

The guys on the football team kept stopping by to talk to Tim and Trent. They tried to include me in the conversation, but I didn't have much to say about football.

When the band played an old favorite of mine, I started to sing along and sway to the music. The next thing I knew Trent turned to Tim. "Mind if I dance with your date?"

"No, of course not," Tim said. "But it's her you have to ask, not me."

Trent held out his hand. "May I have this dance?"

For a second I wondered if Renee would mind. I looked around for her. "She won't care. She hardly knows I exist," Trent laughed.

How did he know what I was thinking? "Besides, we'll just say I was following your mother's request that I dance with you."

I grinned. He was right. Renee couldn't care less. Brian was the only thing on her mind tonight.

Trent was a wonderful dancer. He was so smooth that I felt like I was floating with him. His strong arms held me tight, but not too close. I liked the way I felt next to him. When the first song ended, a fast one began. I started back to my chair. Trent grabbed my arm. "Stay," he commanded.

I obeyed without question. He began to move to the rhythm of the music. I did, too. I followed his lead and we danced to the music. He was wonderful. I grinned at him a lot. He smiled back. Sweat covered his forehead and at one point he flung off his jacket, loosened his tie, and really let himself feel the music.

When the song ended we both clapped and then collapsed in our chairs.

"Hey, Trent, that was great. Where'd you learn to dance like that?" I asked.

"Back home. There's a place we hung out a lot that had real good music."

"Too bad my foot's out of commission. I'd like to learn that last step you were doing," Tim said.

"Yeah, do you like to dance?" Trent asked Tim.

"Tim dances real well," I blurted out. I was feeling disloyal to Tim and felt I had to say something.

"Is that right?" Trent said. "I should have suspected those quick moves out on the field came from somewhere." Then the conversation turned to football and how being quick on your feet is such an asset and how a good football player can be good dancer if he wants to be.

Renee found her way back to our table about eleven o'clock. I knew from the look on her face something was wrong.

"What's up?" I asked her.

"Some nerve she has. I'd like to give her a piece of my mind."

"Sandy?"

"You got it. Do you know what she's saying?"

"No, I haven't talked to her."

"She told Sheila she's going to wear Brian's fraternity pin when he gets it after pledge week."

"I don't believe it. She's dreaming."

"Why do you say that?"

"Renee, haven't you noticed the way Brian looks at you?"

"Looks at me? How?"

"Oh, come on. Brian's still in love with you. It's obvious."

"If it's so obvious, what do you call that?" She pointed to the dance floor. Sandy and Brian were dancing cheek-to-cheek.

"You danced like that with Trent yourself earlier. Brian is probably jealous. Why don't you try talking to him alone?"

"She hasn't left his side for a second."

"Then maybe you should call him at home tomorrow before he leaves."

"She's staying at his house. I couldn't do that." Her face clouded over and tears sprang to her eyes. "Just the thought of those two sitting on *our* couch just makes me want to scream."

"Hey, take it easy. Don't think about that now. Try to relax and have a good time. Trent's a real nice guy."

"I know. You're right." She brushed the tears from her eyes and smiled at me. "Let's get out of here. What do you say?"

I wanted to dance once more with Trent, but couldn't figure out how to pull it off, so leaving was fine with me.

"Let's go to Sharvin Heights," Renée suggested as soon as we were in the car.

I couldn't believe she suggested a trip to the Heights, the most popular makeout spot for twenty miles. I certainly didn't want to go there with Tim. And I knew I couldn't stand to watch Trent kiss Renée.

"Sounds good." Trent turned toward the Heights entrance road. Obviously he knew where he was going, but why was I surprised? No doubt he and Renée had already been there several times. Jealousy flooded through me.

The place was mobbed when we got there. Everyone was in a real party mood. Rich sauntered up to the car as soon as we parked. Renee rolled down her window.

"Hi, everybody," Rich said to all of us. "How about a drink?" He shoved a bottle of wine through the car window.

"Oh, thanks." Renee took a swallow and passed it to Trent.

"No, thanks." He waved the bottle away.

"Tim, Jeannie?" Renee passed the bottle back to us. Tim took it. I shook my head no. I wasn't a drinker. Sam had cured me of that. Sam had tried to drown his problems in a bottle. It hadn't worked. I didn't want to ever again get involved with a drinker. I was glad that Trent had passed the bottle.

"Trent, don't you want a drink?" Renee asked.

"Training, you know."

"I forgot. You don't mind if I do?" She reached for the bottle.

"Be my guest," Trent answered her.

"How was the dance?" Rich wanted to know.

"Boring," Renee answered for all of us.

"I heard Brian was there," Rich said.

"Yup."

Why did Rich have to bring that up?

"Got himself a blonde too, I hear," Rich said. Why didn't he just drop it?

"Rich, have you seen Jeb?" I wanted to change the subject.

"Oh, sure. He's over there with his greaser pals." He pointed across the lot.

"Want to go see them?" I asked Tim. Then I remembered his ankle.

"We could maybe find a parking spot over there," Trent suggested.

"Yeah, let's," I said.

69

"Let's stay here," Renee suggested.

I knew Renee preferred Rich and his friends, but if they were going to talk about Brian that could cause problems. Jeb and the guys on the other side of the park didn't wear designer jeans and listen to the right kind of music, but they had heart and I liked that. Renee needed some understanding tonight, not a hard time from insensitive people.

"Yeah, I agree with Renee. This spot's fine," Tim said.

"You sure?" Renee turned to Tim. "I know you used to hang with that crowd."

"A long time ago. I drifted away from them once I made the football team."

I'd first met Tim at Jeb's house. Tim had been fascinated with Sam. Of course he'd been quick to point out that if I were smart I'd stay away from Sam. I hadn't taken his advice, though.

"Pass that bottle back here, will you?" Tim reached for the wine. "Since I can't play football for a while, I guess I don't have to be in training." Tim emptied the bottle.

Please don't get drunk, I wanted to plead, but I didn't say a word.

"Got any more of this?" Tim asked Rich.

"Yeah, that was good stuff," Renee added.

"Sure do. In the car. Come on over. Join the party." About ten kids milled around Rich's car drinking and talking and laughing. Music blared from a boom box propped on the hood.

"Good idea. It's a little cramped in here." Tim didn't have a lot of room to stretch his leg. I was relieved he didn't want to sit in the car and make out. I wasn't thrilled about joining Rich's friends, but I followed along. Trent didn't have a lot to say, but he stayed near Renee.

Across the way I saw Jeb leaning against his car talking to Steve Laneron. Tim was talking football again, so I wandered over.

"Hi, Jeb, Steve."

"Hey, Jeannie. How's it going?"

"All right."

"Been to the dance, I see." Jeb pointed to my dress. "You look real good."

"Thanks." I knew Jeb meant it. I liked him for being able to tell me.

"Went with Tim, huh?"

I nodded yes.

"And Renee's with the dude?"

"The dude?" Was he referring to Trent?

"Yeah, him." Steve pointed toward Trent.

I laughed. "Why the dude?"

"The boots. And the way he walks."

Trent did have a distinctive walk. I should have known Jeb and his pals would have a comment about that.

"He's really very nice."

"Sure, Jeannie, if you say so."

Jeb didn't believe me, and I wanted him to.

"Speaking of the dude, here he comes."

I turned and saw Trent walking our way. My heart did a flip-flop. Neither Renee nor Tim was following.

Chapter 8

"Hi," Trent said to everyone, but he smiled at me.

"Hi," I answered. "Trent, do you know my friend Jeb?"

"No, I don't. Nice to meet you." He stretched his hand toward Jeb.

"And this is Steve."

He shook hands with him, too.

We all stood in awkward silence. It felt strange to have these guys together.

Finally Jeb said, "You play football, huh?"

"Yeah, a little." Trent wasn't a bragger. I liked that about him. Jeb and his buddies weren't into football, but I loved Jeb for trying to get a conversation going.

"Nice car." Trent pointed to Jeb's restored Chevy. He was so proud of that car.

"You like it?" Jeb smiled.

Trent had said the right thing.

"I sure do. Who did the work?"

"I did." I could hear the pride in Jeb's voice.

"No kidding. It's beautiful." Trent did a slow inspection of the car. He ran his hands over the shiny surface.

"You into cars?" Jeb asked Trent.

"A little. My grandpa has a Packard sitting in his garage he wants to restore."

"What kind of shape is it in?"

"Pretty good, I think. Would you be interested in taking a look at it?"

"Sure, but would your grandpa want me to?"

"Once he sees the job you did on this, I know he will."

"Where do you live?"

"On Oak Boulevard."

Jeb's face turned from interest to indifference. Oak Boulevard was "Rich Kid Row." Jeb didn't have a lot of respect for money. At least that's what he wanted people to think.

"You live on Oak Boulevard, huh? Who's your grandpa?"

"Charlie Minion. You know him?"

"I've heard of him." I saw the set look on Jeb's face. I wanted to scream at him to give Trent a chance. So what if his grandparents had money?

"Grandpa wants to tinker with the car himself, but doesn't know where to start. He's afraid that if he asks the guys he knows they'll take over and do it all. Grandpa is determined to do this himself."

"So you think he'd want someone like me to help him?"

"Why not? Once he gets a look at the work you do, I'm sure he will."

"Hey, pal, you're dreaming. Your rich granddaddy isn't going to want a kid from the wrong side of the tracks messing with his precious Packard."

The force of Jeb's anger startled us all.

"It was just an idea." Trent immediately backed off. "If you'd like to look at it sometime, give me a call. I better see how Renee's doing. Take it easy, everybody.''

Trent smiled at me and walked away.

"What was that all about? The guy was just trying to be friendly." I was furious with Jeb for being so rude.

"Friendly, nothing. I can smell his kind a mile away. If he lives on Rich Kid Row he can afford the best mechanic in town. Don't kid me. He's not going to be interested in having me look at his precious car.''

"Jeb, you're paranoid. You know that? Trent wouldn't have suggested it if he didn't think it was a good idea. I doubt Trent or his grandfather cares where you live.''

"You're so naive, Jeannie. Money matters. Believe me, I know.''

"Maybe you do. But maybe this time you're wrong about somebody.''

"Wrong about him? I doubt it. Look at who he's with. He and Renee make a good pair, don't they? Both with their fancy clothes and souped-up cars.''

"For your information Trent doesn't even have a car. Give the guy a chance.''

I wanted Jeb to like Trent. I felt terrible that this first meeting had bombed. I guess I was always looking for Jeb's approval when it came to the guys I was interested in. But that was silly. Sam had been Jeb's best friend. No one was ever going to fill Sam's shoes as far as Jeb was concerned. Besides, did I really think I'd ever get a date with Trent anyway?

"Okay, maybe I'll give him a chance. And I think he'd like to give you something, too.''

"What's that supposed to mean?''

"That guy is hot for you. I can smell it."

"You don't know what you're talking about. He's going with Renee."

"Big deal. He may be with Renee tonight, but not for long."

"Oh, Jeb."

"Want to make a little wager, J.T.?"

He hadn't called me that in a while. And I didn't like the tone he was using, either. "No," I said, hoping he was right. But how could I do that to my best friend?

I wandered back toward Tim. He and Renee were laughing and sharing the wine bottle. He put his arm around my neck and gave me a slobbery kiss on the cheek. I tried to be enthusiastic, but it was difficult.

A few minutes later, I looked at my watch and faked a yawn.

"I think I better get home."

"It's early, relax."

"Not for me. I have to work tomorrow."

"You do? Maybe I'll come see you," Tim suggested.

"Please don't. The boss doesn't like it when our friends come to visit." I didn't want Tim to get the wrong impression either. This was just a casual date. I wasn't interested in anything serious. "Really, I have to go. Renee, you ready?"

"Sure."

Her answered surprised me. Renee was never ready to go. I wondered what was up.

The ride home was quiet. Tim tried to kiss me a few times, but I managed to discourage anything more. The smell of wine was heavy on his breath.

Renee snuggled close to Trent and whispered in his ear. Once she reached up and kissed him on the cheek. I couldn't stand it. Right then I vowed never again to double-date with them. The torture of Trent not being with me was too much.

Tim insisted on walking me to the door even though I told him he didn't have to.

When he kissed me, I kissed him back and then smiled, trying to be polite. "Good night, Tim. Thanks. I had a good time." With Trent especially, I thought.

"I'll call you tomorrow."

"I have to work, remember?"

"Then Monday."

He hobbled back to the car. Tim might call, but it wouldn't matter. Even though he was nice, I knew he wasn't the guy for me.

The next morning when I came down to the kitchen Mom was drinking coffee and reading the Sunday paper.

"Hi, you're up early," I said. Generally Mom stayed in bed on Sunday morning with the paper spread all over the bed.

"Couldn't sleep. How was the dance?"

"It was okay."

"Just okay?"

I nodded.

"Did you have a good time with Tim?"

"He was all right."

"All right doesn't sound very enthusiastic."

"Tim's really a nice guy, but he's just not for me, that's all."

"Then you'll find somebody else. What about Renee and Trent? Did they have a good time?"

"I guess so."

"Trent seemed nice."

"He is."

"So good-looking and so polite."

I didn't answer.

76

"Does Renee like him a lot?"

"She's still in love with Brian."

"I'm not surprised. They were together for a long time."

"And Brian likes her, too. He couldn't keep his eyes off her last night."

"He did come home for the dance, then?"

"Yeah, with this girl who was a real stuck-up snob."

"Maybe you just don't know her."

"And I don't care to, either."

"Did Renee talk to Brian?"

"Barely. I suggested she call him, but she said no way. They're both so stubborn, I can't believe it."

"At least she has Trent."

"Yeah."

"Why do I get the feeling you don't like that?"

"Because she doesn't appreciate him. I realized last night it's Brian she cares about, not Trent. She's kind of leading him on. That bothers me."

"Why? He must like her if he dates her."

"I know."

"Jeannie, what's going on here? Do I detect a little jealousy?"

I blushed. Mom had a knack for zeroing in on my feelings.

"You know, I thought I sensed something between you two when he came to the door."

"Oh, you did not."

"I did. Why are you trying to deny it?"

"Because Renee is my best friend. I can't like the same guy she does."

"You can't?"

"No. She needs him right now."

"That may be true, but does that mean you have to deny how you feel?"

"What good does it do if I admit it? I can't do anything about it."

"Does not admitting it make the feeling go away?"

"No . . . yes . . . I don't know."

"Oh, Jeannie. I know you don't want to hurt Renee, but if you really do like Trent, then denying it won't make the feeling disappear."

"But how can I like my best friend's boyfriend?"

"Probably because there's something special about him."

"I guess I'm admitting it, huh, Mom?"

"I guess so."

"But what difference does it make? I don't want to upset Renee."

"I know you don't. Maybe you should talk to Renee. Tell her how you feel."

"How can I do that? If only Brian would apologize to Renee. I know she'd forgive him. I just know it."

"And then Trent would be available?"

"Maybe. Oh, Mom, I don't know what to do. But if I don't get moving, I'll be late for work." I gulped the last of my orange juice.

"Want a ride?"

"No, I'll walk. The fresh air will clear my head."

On the way to the station I thought about what Mom had said. She'd sensed something between us and so had Jeb. Was it that obvious? But why was Trent so attentive to Renee? He must like her or he wouldn't go out with her. Trent didn't strike me as the type who did anything he didn't want to.

About noon Renee pulled into the station and came up to the booth. "I have to talk to you."

"I can't. I'm working. You know Mr. Nolan's rules."

"I know, so I'll get my car washed."

"Get in line, then."

Renee gave the starter her keys, smiled at him, and convinced him to drive her car through the line so she could talk to me while her car was being washed. She came back to the booth.

"It's true. He's going to give her his fraternity pin."

"How do you know?"

"I talked to him last night. After I dropped Trent off I stopped at Arly's. They were there."

"That's why you were so eager to leave the Heights. I should have known."

"And we got into this awful fight."

"What happened?"

"When I walked into Arly's they were sitting in a booth near the door. I said hello and Brian suggested I sit with them because all the booths were taken."

"Did you?"

"I would have, but Sandy said, 'Brian, honey, let's just let her have the booth. I'm tired. I'd like to go.'"

"So you dumped your Coke on that long blonde hair of hers?"

"I wanted to. But I didn't because Brian ignored her and asked me about the new routine he heard we'd done at the game. Sandy didn't like it one bit. The whole time she kept hanging on him and touching his arm and looking at him in this sick way. I wanted to throw up."

"And Brian ignored her?"

"Yes, it was wonderful. He just kept talking to me and asking me questions. I loved it."

"If everything was so wonderful what was the fight about?"

"When I asked him when he was going back to school, he said early today because pledge week starts tonight, and Sandy pipes up and says, 'When Brian gets his fraternity pin I'm going to wear it!' I looked at Brian waiting for him to deny it."

"Did he?"

"No, so finally I asked him straight out, and he nodded yes."

I couldn't understand why he'd do that. It was so clear he still liked Renee.

"You should have seen her gloating," Renee continued. "It was disgusting. That's when I got up and ran to my car. But before I got to it, Brian stopped me. He took my arm, but I shoved him away and screamed at him never to touch me again. Then I screamed a few other things at him like he was a two-faced jerk and I never loved him and I didn't care what he did or who he did it with. I told him he could rot in hell before I'd ever talk to him again. He kept saying, 'Renee, I'm sorry.' So I asked him why, if he was so sorry, he was going to give Sandy his pin. He said because he thought I didn't care about him. I told him he was right, I didn't. Then I jumped into my car and got out of there as fast as I could. I cried all the way home and half the night. Oh, Jeannie, I feel so miserable."

"I can imagine. What an awful scene. I don't get it, though. The way he looked at you at the dance sure seemed real to me."

"You were seeing things, Jeannie. He doesn't care. She's probably easy, and he loves it."

"Oh, come on."

"It's true."

"Renee, don't do that to yourself. You told me a hundred times Brian liked you because you were honest enough to tell him you weren't ready for any heavy-duty action.''

"I guess he didn't mean it. Looks to me like as soon as he got the chance, he took it."

"I don't believe that, and neither do you. Hey, your car's done. Want to come back later so we can talk?"

"I guess. Nobody except a friend like you would listen to me."

"Listen, I get off at 5:30. Why don't you stop by then and we'll talk it out?"

"Okay, I will. But meanwhile I'm going to think of every torture humanly possible to inflict on that creep. How could this happen to me?" Renee's eyes filled with tears.

"I'm sorry. I know how much you're hurting."

"Hey, it's not your fault. See you later."

When Renee drove away I felt sick to my stomach. I'd been counting on Brian and Renee to come to their senses. If they didn't, there was no way I could ever tell Renee how much I liked Trent. She would put me in the same category as Sandy. I didn't know who to be mad at. Sandy for stealing Brian, Brian for being so weak, or myself for wanting something I couldn't have.

Chapter 9

The afternoon dragged by because I was tired and depressed. About three o'clock I went on break. I was sitting on the curb under a tree sipping a Diet Coke when Tim pulled up in his mother's car. He was the last person I wanted to see.

"What are you doing driving with a sprained ankle?" I said, trying to sound concerned rather than annoyed.

"It's my left foot that's hurt. Since this is an automatic, I convinced my mom I can drive just fine with my right foot."

"Oh." I didn't want to deal with him. I had enough on my mind as it was.

"Good mood, huh?" Tim said.

I shrugged my shoulders.

"Working on Sunday is a bummer. How about going to Arly's when you get off work?"

"No thanks. Renee's coming by for me."

"Then we'll all go. Renee's a good time. That would be fun. And I'll even buy."

"Thanks, but I don't think so. Renee's kind of down." So was I, but not for the reasons he thought.

"Oh, sure. Brian, I suppose. How he could treat Renee that way is beyond me. She's terrific. He must have rocks in his cranium."

"I agree." Boy, did I agree.

"And you two probably want to talk. Right?"

"Something like that."

"I understand. I sure had a good time last night."

I didn't answer right away. But I knew it was time to tell it to Tim straight.

"The dance was fun." Because of Trent, I wanted to say. "But Tim, I don't want you to get the wrong idea. You're really sweet but I'm not interested in anything serious. I just want you to know that."

"What are you saying, Jeannie?"

"I'm saying you and I are different. You enjoy drinking with the gang and hanging around. I don't."

"You didn't seem to be bored last night at the Heights."

"I wasn't. It was fine, really. I just don't want you thinking there is something more between us than there really is."

"Oh, I get it. You want to date around. Is that it?"

Not around, just Trent, I wanted to shout at him.

"I think I'm not the person for you. That's all."

"Jeannie, why don't you just tell it to me straight. I'm not the person for you."

"What's the difference? I don't think it would work. That's all."

"B.S., Jeannie. Just admit it. You want me out of the way so you can move in on Trent."

"What are you talking about?"

"You know what I'm talking about. But how will you explain it to your best friend?"

"You're out of your mind."

"No I'm not. I saw you and Trent last night. So did everybody else. Dancing, talking. It was obvious."

"What was obvious?" My heart was pounding.

83

"He's hot for you too, kid. Good luck." Tim started to pull away.

"Tim, wait."

"Why? I get the message. I can take a hint."

"I'm sorry," I cried after him.

"Tell that to Renee," Tim called as his car squealed away.

I went back to work, my mind spinning from his words. Jeb, my mother, and now Tim. Were my feelings for Trent that obvious?

I was relieved to have set Tim straight about him and me, but I was confused about his comments. Was Tim right? Did Trent like me as much as I liked him? I desperately wanted him to. I didn't want to hurt Renee, but I also wanted Trent. He was the first guy since Sam who had made me feel alive and happy. I had tried to deny it, but there was no denying it anymore. Maybe the best thing I could do was talk to Renee. I didn't think she really liked him anyway. She was always telling me to find somebody I liked. I bet she would be happy for me. Finally I decided that I would talk to her. When she came to pick me up after work, I'd just be honest with her. I'd tell her how I felt. We were best friends. We could handle it. I wanted to believe it would be all right.

The entrance to the car wash closed at five, but there were still cars in line to be washed. While I waited for them to finish, I organized the work schedule for the week after next. I was so absorbed in juggling the schedule that I didn't hear him approach the booth.

"Hey, lady, can I get my car washed?"

I jumped at the voice, sure I was dreaming. I wasn't. Trent was leaning against the glass.

"What?"

"This is a car wash, isn't it?"

"Yes." I was so happy to see him. I wanted to run out of the booth and throw my arms around him.

He shoved a ten through the slot. "I want my car washed, please."

"I didn't know you had a car."

"I borrowed one." He pointed at a gleaming blue Chrysler.

"That needs washing?" It certainly did not. The shine on it was enough to give one eyestrain.

"You don't think so?"

"No." Then I couldn't help myself. I grinned at him. "Besides the car wash closes at five. See the sign?" I motioned toward the posted hours.

He looked at me for the longest time. I felt his eyes looking deep within me.

"What are you doing here, Trent?"

"I wanted to see you."

My stomach lurched. My mouth went dry. I stared at him. He stared right back. Finally I found my voice.

"I'm glad. I wanted to see you, too." I looked deep into his blue eyes. There was nothing else to say. We both let the moment be. I knew then he felt the same way I did. Best friend or not, Trent and I were meant to be.

A car horn jarred me back to reality. Renee's Mustang pulled into the station. Trent saw her just as she saw him. I fumbled with the last of the cash and shoved it in the safe.

Out of the corner of my eye I saw Renee get out of her car and come toward the booth.

"Hi," she said.

"Hello, Renee," Trent said. I couldn't see if he smiled at her.

"I'm just about done." I tried to be perky.

"No hurry. How'd you know I'd be here?" Renee asked Trent.

"I didn't."

"Then what are you doing here?"

"I came to see Jeannie," Trent answered. I just wanted to die. I felt so guilty. Didn't Trent?

"To see Jeannie?" Renee sounded confused. She looked to me for an explanation. I looked away, my face turning red. Why did I feel so guilty when I wasn't doing anything wrong?

Doubt clouded Renee's face. "Did you say you came to see Jeannie?"

"Yeah." Trent looked at me and smiled.

My heart ached for Renee. My heart soared for me.

"Ready to go?" I asked Renee as I locked the door and set the burglar alarm. Tonight it was my job to lock up. Mr. Nolan would come by later and recheck everything. I decided I'd better talk to Renee right away. I prayed she'd understand.

"Sure." Renee started toward her car. I followed.

"I'll call you," Trent said. We both turned. He was looking straight at me.

"Okay . . ." The words died in Renee's throat. A glimmer of understanding crossed her eyes.

"And I'll call you, too," he said to Renee.

"Wrong, wrong, wrong," she screamed at him. "Don't bother."

"We need to talk, Renee," Trent said.

"No, we don't. We have nothing to say."

"Renee, don't do this," I begged her.

She turned on me. "Renee, don't do this? Are you

crazy? You steal him right from under my nose and you tell me don't do this? What's wrong with you?"

"Renee, listen to me."

"Listen to what? Excuses. First Brian deserts me and now you dump on me. And you, you jerk," looking at Trent, "aren't even worth talking about."

"Renee, I know you're upset, but face it, I was just a temporary replacement for Brian. That was pretty clear last night at the dance."

"It was, huh?"

"Yes, it was. We were both using each other, and it isn't working, so it's best to just let it go," Trent said.

"I'm going to let it go all right. You both can go to hell for all I care."

"Renee, stop it," I pleaded.

"Here I thought you were my friend. Here I thought you were telling me straight about Brian. Boy, what a fool I was. All you cared about was getting him. You don't care about me. You never did."

"That's not true. I care about you very much. You're my best friend. I love you."

"Sure, I can tell. See you around." Renee jumped in her car and started the engine. I tried to stop her from leaving, but she wouldn't even look at me.

"Let her go," Trent said, grabbing my arm and stopping me from running into the street when she sped away.

I turned to Trent, the anguish I felt leaping from me.

"We can't do anything for her right now." He held my hand tight.

"I suppose you're right. I just feel so awful."

"I know. I do too. But she's going to have to get through this on her own."

87

"I feel like I'm deserting her. She's stuck by me in some pretty rough times."

"And you'll be there for her when she's ready."

We watched her car disappear around the corner.

"How about we get something to eat? We can talk, too," Trent suggested.

"All right, but I have to call home first."

Trent was waiting in the car when I finished using the phone.

"Want to go to Arly's?" he suggested.

"No, I don't think so."

"Probably not a good idea. How about the Burger King on 9th Street?"

"That sounds good." I wanted to be as far away from Renee and Tim and all the gossip as possible. As happy as I was to be with Trent, I had the same feeling I often had with Sam. I shouldn't be with him. Nobody approved. I pushed the feeling away, not wanting to deal with that.

We tried to kid around and make jokes, but neither of us felt much like laughing. After we ate, we drove out to the country. Another reminder of what Sam and I so often did.

We pulled off the road and parked under a giant oak tree. "What did you mean when you said you and Renee were both using each other? I know what she was doing, but what about you?" I asked him.

"I wanted to meet people fast, make friends, be accepted. Renee served that purpose real well. She knows everybody. She's popular. As long as I was with her, I had lots of friends."

"I'm not nearly as outgoing as Renee. If you give her up, things will be different. Are you sure you want to do that?"

"I'm sure. You're far more my type than Renee. I've known that a long time."

"What type am I?"

"The type who thinks a good time is a drive in the country and a nice slow dance, among other things."

Remembering the feel of my body against his at the dance sent chills through me. I hoped he was remembering the same thing. I looked at him and smiled. His hand gently lifted my chin and he leaned over to kiss me. Before our lips ever met, my body was on fire. When our skin touched, I felt his warm, moist, eager lips match mine. I pulled away, took his face in my hands, and let myself look deep into those tender eyes. I wanted him to see what I was feeling. I saw I was not alone.

We talked and talked that night. There was so much to say, so much to learn, so much to hear. For a little while Renee's unhappiness faded and I lost myself in loving someone new.

Chapter 10

I spent a restless night thinking about Renee. I hadn't meant to hurt her. I didn't want to betray her. Somehow I had to figure out a way to get her to understand what had happened. It wasn't going to be easy.

Monday morning I left for school early. I watched for Renee, hoping she would come by to pick me up, but not really expecting her to. All the way to school I watched for her Mustang. When I arrived at school, her car was already in the parking lot. I figured she'd come to school early to avoid running into me.

Renee usually came by my locker before first period. She liked to breeze up and down the halls saying hello to everyone. Five minutes before the first bell I saw her making her rounds. Sheila was with her.

When Renee sauntered past my locker, she didn't even look my way. But I called to her.

"Renee." She ignored me and kept walking. I called again. "Renee." She still didn't respond. I hurried after her and grabbed her arm to get her attention. "Renee, could I talk to you a second?"

She spun around. "I believe your hand is on me. Please remove it." She was pure ice.

Humiliated, I jerked my hand away.

Her icy stare shot through me and she turned away.

"Renee, please," I begged.

"Leave me alone, traitor."

My whole body stiffened. I felt like I'd been slapped. Shame, then anger poured through my body. I watched them walk away.

"What happened?" Trent was beside me. "You look awful. Maybe you better sit down." He edged me toward the lockers and tried to get me to sit down. I backed up, but my knees wouldn't bend. I pushed his arm away.

"I'm all right," I managed to say. Finally I looked at him. Love and concern filled his eyes. It took away some of the pain of Renee's snub.

"What happened?"

I pointed down the hall toward Renee's retreating back.

"She won't even talk to me." Tears brimmed my eyes. I fought to keep them at bay.

"She's upset now. But she'll come around. You wait and see. I'll talk to her later. She'll calm down."

"Do you really think so?" I wanted to believe him.

"Sure. She's humiliated and angry right now. Besides, it's Brian she's really upset with, not you or me."

"It sure feels like it's me."

"I know. But just hang in there. It'll be all right."

His reassurance helped. I wanted him to be right.

"See you at lunch?" Trent lifted my chin and grinned at me.

"Sure." I smiled back. He was so beautiful.

At lunch I found a seat in the corner near the door

and watched for Trent, relieved Renee and I didn't have the same lunch period. I couldn't deal with another attack from her. Sometimes I sat with Sheila and her friends, but since she'd been with Renee this morning I knew whose side she was on.

I sensed I was being watched. When I looked toward Sheila's table, they all quickly looked away. I wanted to die. Trent still hadn't come, and I felt so conspicuous.

About fifteen minutes into the lunch period Trent came through the door, looking upset. He bought his lunch and carried his tray over to my table. The room buzzed when he joined me.

He tried to smile, but it was forced.

"What's wrong?"

"Nothing."

"Trent, please, let's not start out that way. If we can't be honest, it's not going to work."

"I suppose you're right. I just talked to Renee."

"And?"

"And maybe I was wrong. Maybe she isn't going to come around."

"Why? What did she say?"

"Basically she called me every name she could think of—the politest was a low-down rotten, conniving, two-timing jerk. She wouldn't even listen to what I was trying to say."

"She's like that when she's angry. That's partly why she and Brian can't get back together."

"I sure hope she calms down eventually."

"Do you still think it's Brian she's mad at and not us?"

"Of course. We both know she's in love with him, not me. But he isn't here to get angry at, and we are."

"Brian is a jerk too. I'm so mad at him right now."

"Me too. I don't understand him. He sure didn't seem that wild about Sandy."

"I don't think he is. My guess is Brian can't stand not having an adoring female hanging around. And Sandy's available."

"He's that insecure?" Trent asked.

"Apparently. Maybe I should talk to him."

"Why?"

"To persuade him to try to talk to Renee again."

"Do you think that would work?"

"I don't know. I got the feeling on Saturday he wanted to talk to me, but we were never alone."

"It might be worth a try. If Renee could get the mess with Brian straightened out, maybe we could get us straightened out."

"I know."

"Do you get the feeling we're being watched?" Trent suddenly asked.

"Yeah, apparently Renee has already had plenty to say about us."

"And obviously she's been very persuasive. The air in here is frigid."

"You don't mind being unpopular, do you?"

"No. Not over this. I know we didn't do anything wrong."

"Thanks." I sure didn't want Trent to resent me for causing him to lose all his friends. But I knew he wasn't being completely honest. He did care about what people thought.

I wanted to reach out and pull him to me. I could see the anguish in his face in spite of his words. I didn't want him to be hurting even for a second. If he was in pain, so was I.

"It's not that simple, Jeannie."

"What do you mean?"

"It's a long story. We'll talk about it later."

I had no idea what he was talking about. The bell rang and there was a scramble for the door before I could ask him what he meant. Jeb and Steve were on their way in the cafeteria as we were leaving.

I smiled at them. "Hi, guys."

Jeb looked at the two of us together. I could tell he was trying not to say I told you so. He simply nodded to us.

"What's with him?" Trent asked after Jeb passed.

"What do you mean?"

"He's so protective of you. Why?"

"We've been through a lot together. Sometime I'll tell you all about it."

"Does it have to do with that boyfriend of yours who killed himself playing chicken?"

"Sam didn't kill himself. It was an accident. Where did you hear that, anyway?" My body stiffened.

"Renee told me."

"She said Sam killed himself?" Renee wouldn't have said that.

"Not exactly, but from the story she told me, it sounded like that."

"Well, he didn't kill himself. I should know."

"Of course you do. Listen, I'm sorry. I don't want to fight about this."

"Me either. We have enough to worry about. I'll see you later." I left Trent in the middle of the corridor. I wasn't sure what had upset me. I suppose it was reasonable to think Sam had killed himself, but he hadn't. Someday I'd tell Trent the whole story.

*   *   *

94

Work was slow, typical for a Monday. But I managed to keep busy juggling the schedule and balancing last week's books. Mr. Nolan was in a bad mood. One guy hadn't shown up for work and another had called in sick.

"All these people complaining about being out of work, and then when I hire them they don't show up. I don't get it. I really don't. And then when they do show up, I have to watch them every second so they don't cheat me. Just once I'd like to catch one of my employees skimming. I'd throw the thief in the slammer so quickly he wouldn't know what hit him."

I didn't answer. Mr. Nolan often talked tough and I had learned he was talking more to himself than me. Theft was a real problem. Both money and supplies disappeared too fast. But Mr. Nolan trusted me, so he said a lot of things he wouldn't to the other employees. Mostly I listened when he complained.

Near quitting time, I found myself automatically watching for Renee, who always picked me up on Mondays. I wondered if she ever would again. Already I missed her. I wanted so much to talk to her, to be able to call her on the phone when I got home, but that wasn't possible. My heart ached for the loneliness creeping through me.

The next morning, Jeb was slouched in his seat when I got to my first-hour class.

"You okay?" I asked him.

"Yeah," he mumbled.

"Trouble at home again?" Jeb had talked his dad into letting him back in the house. Maybe that had been a mistake.

"Yeah, the old man finally told Ma he wasn't ever going back to the factory. Tried to make it sound like it was his decision, but she figured it out. Then they had a big argument. I just wish he could find a job.''

"Does he have any leads?"

"Not really. He wants a job that pays as much as the factory did, and that's never going to happen."

"Hey, I don't know if he's interested, but Mr. Nolan is looking for people."

"At the car wash?"

"Yeah. It doesn't pay a lot, but it's a job."

"I'll tell him, but I can hear him already. 'Me, washing cars, you crazy, boy?'"

"Forget it, then."

"No, I'll tell him. If I thought I could handle it, I'd apply."

"You're already working full-time. I don't know how you do it now." Jeb worked long hours at a body shop on 9th Street.

"It isn't easy, but I manage. The bad part is that our savings are gone. I give Mom my check every week, but it doesn't even pay the rent."

I knew Jeb had always taken money home. I didn't know he gave it all to his parents. No wonder he never had much money. His family loyalty puzzled me. It seemed to me his parents took advantage of him. And the fights with his dad were hard for me to think about. Dad had slapped me once freshman year when I came in late after being with Sam. That was the only time he'd ever hit me. He apologized later and vowed it would never happen again. He'd kept his promise, too.

Trent was waiting for me after class.

"You still talking to me?"

"Of course. I'm sorry I stomped off like that. I guess I'm just a little touchy when it comes to Sam. Sorry."

"That's okay. The truth is I think I'm jealous."

"Of what?" Trent, jealous? What was he talking about?

"Of Sam. Renee told me how much you loved him and how there hasn't been a guy since you've really cared about. I think you're still hung up on him."

"I don't think hung up is the word. Sure I loved him, but that was a long time ago, Trent. I don't want to live my whole life in the past. Renee may be right, I haven't been interested in any one guy since Sam, but that's different now. Now I've met you."

"Are you sure?"

"I'm positive. Besides, I suspect there's a lot of your past you haven't shared with me, too. You can't tell me this gorgeous face of yours hasn't attracted a girl or two."

"I hope it isn't just my face you're interested in."

"Definitely not." Then I blushed. "It's your mind I'm interested in." I stammered to cover the images that crossed my mind.

"Good." We both laughed.

"And what exactly is it you're interested in?" I asked him.

"Your body." He grinned.

"If that's all, then I'm taking a hike. There are plenty of guys around for that."

"And your mind too, of course."

I had to laugh. Being with Trent was so easy.

We met again for lunch. It was a beautiful October day. The sun was shining and the breeze was gentle. We gobbled our hamburgers and wandered out to the Circle. Lots of other kids had the same idea.

Renee was sitting on the grass near the fountain. Why wasn't she in class? She stared at us as we made our way across the Circle. I was tempted to go back inside, but I refused to let her determine where I went or what I did.

"Hi, Renee." I smiled at her, but it was an effort. Her coldness gripped me in the pit of my stomach.

"Hello, Renee," Trent said. Tension filled the air.

"Aren't the love birds cute," Renee said to Sheila and the other girls sitting on the lawn. She ignored our greeting.

"Please, Renee, don't start," Trent said. I looked at him, begging him to ignore her.

"You talking to me?" Renee asked.

"Yes, I am."

"Well, I'm not talking to you." She turned her back to us.

"Why not, Renee? What are you afraid of?" Trent asked.

She spun around. I knew Trent's question unhinged her. She stammered trying to think of an answer.

"Come on, Trent. Let's go." I tugged on his arm.

"In a second. She has a right to be angry and hurt, but maybe it's time she at least listened to someone else for a change."

"She'll come around. You said so yourself," I whispered to him.

"Maybe she needs a little help."

"You talking about me?" Renee stood up and stepped toward Trent.

"Yes, I am. I know you're hurt and angry, but you don't need to be cruel. I may not mean anything to you, but what about Jeannie? She's your best friend."

"Not anymore. She's as slimy as you are."

"That kind of talk isn't necessary," Trent said. I wanted to cry.

"Who's going to stop me? The big-shot boy from

98

the city? Why don't you smack me around a little, just like your old man did to your mother, and like you did to your old man.''

The silence was frightening.

"We're talking about you and Jeannie here. Let's leave my family out of it,'' Trent said, barely above a whisper.

"Why? You don't want your sweetie here to know you beat your old man so bad he ended up in the hospital and the only reason you aren't still in jail is because your rich granddaddy bailed you out and that's why you're living here?'' Then she turned to me. "You better be careful, Jeannie. This guy is dangerous, right, Sheila?''

Sheila's face was red. "Renee, stop it,'' she said.

"No, this boy wanted to talk. I'll be happy to talk to them. You know, Jeannie, you got a real knack for picking guys. First you chose Sam who was nothing but a hotheaded drunk, and now you got Trent, who talks with his fists.''

"Cut it out, Renee.'' Trent stepped toward her.

"And if I don't? What are you going to do? Hit me? Go ahead. I'll have you in jail so fast your head will spin.''

"Come on, let's go.'' I tugged on Trent's arm. He backed up slowly. His eyes never left Renee.

On our way to the cafeteria he looked neither to the right nor left. His body was ramrod straight. The things Renee had said raced through my head. Were they true? On Sunday night I'd asked Trent about his family, but he'd put me off. Said we'd talk later.

"You okay?'' I tried to get him to talk to me and look at me.

"Sure. Listen, I have to get something from my locker. See you later.'' He was gone before I could respond.

Chapter 11

Trent disappeared for the rest of the afternoon. After school I waited near the football locker room hoping to catch him before I went to the car wash.

At work I couldn't concentrate, so I took an early supper break and walked back to school. The team was just finishing practice. I didn't spot Trent when the squad filed into the locker room.

I hung around waiting for them to change. The guys came out of the locker room in groups, but Trent wasn't with any of them. I was just about to give up and go back to work when Tim opened the locker room door. I tried to duck around the corner, but he saw me.

"Hey, Jeannie, wait up." Tim limped down the hall after me.

Reluctantly I waited for him. If he was going to give me another lecture I wasn't up for it.

"You looking for Trent?"

I nodded yes.

"He didn't show up for practice. The coach is really streaming about it." Where was he, I wondered? "One of the guys on the team said he wasn't in trig this afternoon, either."

"Maybe he got sick and went home." I didn't

really think so, but I felt like I had to make an excuse for him.

"Yeah, he probably got sick because of what Renee was saying."

"You heard?"

"Are you kidding? The whole school has."

"Renee doesn't know when to shut up sometimes."

"Jeannie, what do you expect? First Brian deserts her, then both you and Trent dump on her."

"Since when are you such a defender of Renee?"

"Since she's needed a friend."

I didn't know what to say. I felt like crying.

"Listen, I'm not saying Renee was right blabbing that story, but considering what she's going through, it's understandable."

"What about what Trent's going through, having a story like that spread about him?"

"I know. But it was bound to get out eventually. Things like that have a way of creeping out."

"Are you saying that what she said is true? I can't believe Trent would do anything like that."

"Well, Sheila told Renee the story. Sheila's mom heard it from Trent's grandmother."

"And she told Renee and Renee announced to the school."

"You got it. Sheila is furious that Renee blabbed it. Her mom is going to kill her, she said."

"She should. But I still can't believe it. Trent just isn't like that. He wouldn't beat up his own father."

"Don't look at me, Jeannie. I learned a long time ago most stories have two sides. Why don't you ask Trent yourself?"

"I'm going to, when I can find him. You know, Tim, I remember you warning me about Sam a few years ago. Are you doing the same thing now?"

101

"Nope. I hope I'm smarter now. Listen, Jeannie. I like you. You know I do. I just don't want to see you get hurt again, that's all."

"Thanks, Tim. I really do appreciate that. Right now I could use some help."

"You got it. Want to take a ride and see if we can find Trent?"

"I wish I could, but I'm on my supper break. I have to be back to work at six." I had only a few more minutes, and with the mood Mr. Nolan was in lately, I didn't dare be late.

"I'll see if I can scout him out. If I find out anything, I'll stop at the car wash."

"Thanks, Tim."

"Meantime, come on. I'll drive you."

Work was a drag. Mr. Nolan was still shorthanded, so he had to work the line himself. About seven o'clock Jeb's father pulled into the car wash. Mr. Nolan stopped working and they talked for a long time. The next thing I knew Mr. Nolan was showing him around the car wash. Mr. Nolan did that only after he hired someone. Part of me was happy for Jeb's dad, but I also hoped he wasn't going to cause trouble. I knew that if he came to work drunk, Mr. Nolan would fire him immediately.

Mr. Nolan was in a much better mood when he came in to close.

"Just hired that fellow over there. I think he's going to work out real good. He caught on fast when I showed him what to do."

"Good," I answered.

"Said he got laid off over at the factory. Said he's given up hope about being called back. With my luck they'll call him back tomorrow."

Just then Jeb's dad came into the office.

Mr. Nolan introduced me. "Jeannie, this is Earl Mitchell. Earl, Jeannie Tanger."

"Hi," I said. I'd met him a couple of times, but I knew he didn't remember me. "I know your son, Jeb," I said.

"Oh, yeah." He was looking all around the office. I wondered what he was so curious about.

"You can go home, Jeannie. I'll lock up," Mr. Nolan said.

"Okay, thanks." Maybe when I got home I'd hear something from Tim.

When I called Mom for a ride, she said she'd be right over. Now that it was dark when I got off work, she didn't like me walking home alone. Renee used to pick me up, but no more.

"Anybody call, Mom?" I asked as soon as I was in the car.

"No. You expecting someone?"

"Not exactly."

"Renee usually picks you up when you work late. She busy tonight?"

"Yeah, she is."

"I haven't seen her lately. What's she so busy doing?"

"Feeling sorry for herself."

"Still pining for Brian, huh?"

"Yeah, something like that."

"You sound like you're mad at her."

I shrugged my shoulders.

"Whatever it is, I'm sure you two can work it out. You've been through some pretty rough times together."

"I hope so, but this time she's acting like a real jerk."

"Does Trent have anything to do with this?"

"I'm afraid so. She's furious with me because she

thinks I stole him from her. The truth is she never had him in the first place.''

"She'll come around. Just give her time."

Everybody said that. I wasn't sure. I decided to change the subject. "Mom, didn't you say you and Dad went to school with Trent's mom?"

"Yes, I did. Why?"

"Did you know the guy she married?"

"No. He wasn't from around here. In fact, that was a real soap opera at the time."

"What was?"

"Their marriage."

"Why?"

"They eloped. Took off in the middle of the night and got married somewhere out West."

"Why'd they elope?"

"Her parents didn't approve of him. He was older than she was. I saw him once. He was a big bruiser of a fellow. And good-looking, too. Of course she was a beauty herself. Well, look at Trent. He got those looks from his parents, that's for sure."

"So she ran off and married him?"

"That's right. And her parents were furious. She didn't come home for years. That's why I was so surprised when Trent said who his grandparents were. As far as I knew she had more or less disappeared. Seldom even came to visit."

"Have you heard any rumors about Trent or his mom since he's been back?"

"Why do you ask?" Mom gave me a funny look.

"Just wondering. Renee was saying some pretty terrible things today about Trent and his family."

"What does Trent say?"

"I haven't had a chance to ask him."

"Well, honey, I'd talk to him before I started

104

listening to rumors. We both know how people like to talk.'' That was the truth.

The phone didn't ring after I got home, and Trent wasn't at school the next morning. I lingered near his locker, but he never showed.

I hoped Jeb would be in a better mood, but he wasn't too happy when he came to class.

"Your dad came to the car wash last night.'' I thought maybe he didn't know.

"I heard. He got a job, huh?''

"Yeah, Mr. Nolan liked him.''

"I hope it lasts.''

"Why, don't you think it will?''

"I don't know. I'm afraid he'll work just long enough to qualify for unemployment and then screw up so he gets fired and can collect unemployment checks.''

"Oh.'' Other people had tried that. Mr. Nolan never fired them, though. He worked them to death and gave them such lousy hours they usually quit before he had to fire them. I decided I'd better not tell Jeb that. "Don't worry about it. I'm sure it'll work out.''

"Say, Jeannie, do you think Trent was serious about me looking at his grandpa's car?''

"I think so. I doubt if he'd have said it if he didn't mean it.''

"Would you ask him?''

"If I ever see him again.''

"What does that mean?''

"Nothing. I'm just talking to myself.''

"I heard the story about Trent. Is it true?''

"I don't know. And he hasn't been around to ask.''

"This place is something, isn't it? People in this

105

school aren't happy unless they've got somebody to talk about. Personally, I can understand completely if Trent belted his old man. I feel like doing that myself sometimes.''

I looked hard at Jeb. Pain covered his face. I wanted to reach out and hug him, but this wasn't the place.

At lunch I was hiding in my usual corner when I saw Trent come into the cafeteria. He bought a hot dog and headed straight for me. Sheila never took her eyes off him.

''May I?'' he asked.

''Captain, may I, isn't it?'' I said.

''Right. Captain, may I sit down and apologize to you?''

''Sure, sit down. Why the apology, though?''

''Because I acted like such a jerk. Walking off like that without an explanation.''

''Hey, you don't owe me an explanation.''

''I know I don't owe you one. But I do want to tell you what Renee was talking about. I wanted to tell you last Sunday, but it's so hard to talk about. Can I pick you up after work and we'll go for a ride?''

''I don't work today. It's my day off.''

''Oh. I've got practice after school, so how about if I come over after supper.''

''Sure. You got a car?''

''I think I can borrow my grandpa's. He's getting better about things like that.''

''That's good.'' I didn't know how things had been, so I wasn't sure what he meant.

''Oh, before I forget, Jeb says if you're serious about him looking at your grandpa's Packard, he'd like to do that.''

''Yeah, I was serious. I'll mention it to Grandpa.''

106

The afternoon dragged by. I just wanted evening to come so I could see Trent.

Dad was in a bad mood at supper.

"Trouble at work, honey?" Mom asked.

"Yeah. The same old problems. I lost last week's pool, too, by just one game." Every week during the fall the men ran a football pool. Dad hated to lose. They had three winners a week and Dad was often one of them.

"Next week, honey, you'll do better."

"Could I be excused?" I asked as soon as I cleared my plate.

"What's the hurry?" Dad asked.

"I'm going out for a little while. I want to get ready."

"You going someplace with Renee?" he asked.

"No. Trent Justin is coming by."

Dad frowned. "I thought he was dating Renee."

"Not anymore."

"Well, where you going? When will you be home?" Dad seldom questioned me. I wondered why all the questions tonight.

"Just for a ride. I'll be home by ten."

"That long?"

"Dad, what's wrong? I did my homework. I won't be late."

"Do you know this guy very well?"

"Well enough. Why?" I felt a little sick to my stomach.

"I just wondered. That's all. This boy is new in town and I want you to be safe."

"Dad, I will be. Why all the questions?"

"I'm your father. I have a right to know where you're going and with whom."

"I know, but you haven't drilled me like this in a long time. Why the sudden interest?"

"Yeah, Al, what's going on?" Even Mom was curious.

"Talk at the factory. You know how it is."

"No, I don't," Mom said.

"I heard a story today that this boy Trent was in a lot of trouble in the city, and that's why his grandpa brought him up here."

"What kind of trouble?" Mom asked.

"I don't know. But I guess if Jeannie says he's okay, it's all right." Dad knew more than he was saying and I knew it. I was glad he was trusting me, but his concern bothered me.

"Yes, he is okay. Now if you'll excuse me." I pushed out my chair, carried my dishes to the sink, and hurried to my room to get ready.

"Al, what's the big mystery?" Mom asked Dad as soon as I left the kitchen.

I never bothered to listen to his answer. Apparently the whole town was gossiping about Trent. Well, I wasn't about to listen to gossip. Trent could tell me what I needed to know.

Chapter 12

From my bedroom window I saw Trent pull up in front of the house. I raced down the stairs. "I'll be home by ten," I called to my parents who were watching television in the living room.

I was out the door and down the front steps before Trent got out of the car.

"Hi." He grinned when he saw me.

"Hi." I smiled back.

Once I was with Trent, I relaxed a little and pushed my nagging doubts away. Trent seemed tense and I wanted him to feel at ease with me.

We drove out to the country and parked in a deserted field.

Trent looked at me for a long time before he said anything.

"You know you're the only one at school who isn't avoiding me like the plague. It's awful."

"I know. I haven't been too popular myself."

"Renee does have a following, doesn't she?"

"Yup. But in the long run the kids will make up their own minds. I found that out about them."

"Because of Sam."

"Yes. People judged him all wrong, but after the accident many of them told me how sorry they were they hadn't given him more of a chance."

"That's good to know. But right now . . . Wow! It's so hard."

"I know. Just hang in there."

"I am. Meantime, I know you're wondering what the real story is."

"Sure, but you don't have to tell me if you don't want to."

"But I do. It's been so hard not having anybody to talk to. For a while Renee was a real distraction, but I knew sooner or later people were bound to find out."

"Find out what?"

"That I got thrown in jail for putting my old man in the hospital."

My heart skipped a beat. So it was true. He had beaten up his father.

"Jeannie, the rumors are true. I did beat him up. I was beating on him so hard, it took two men to drag me off him. I wonder sometimes if I would have stopped if they hadn't made me."

"I bet you would have."

"I'd like to think so. But it's scary remembering how out of control I was. I just couldn't take it anymore."

"Couldn't take what?"

"The way he treated Mom and me. The last couple of years had gotten unbearable. He was always giving Mom a hard time. And he was on my back about everything, too. No matter what I did, it was wrong."

"So you've been fighting a long time?"

"Arguing, but not a knock-out fight like this one. Before it was his attitude. He would say awful, cruel things. He'd come home some nights and yell and scream and call me names and make threats for no

110

reason. Then he'd start in on Mom. I hated that more than anything."

"What did she do?"

"At first she tried to defend herself and me, but we both learned that was useless. Eventually when he started on her she just let him do it."

"Why? Was she afraid of him?"

"I think so. She felt trapped, I guess. That's what Grandma says, anyway."

"Why did she feel trapped?"

"She didn't feel she had anywhere to go. She didn't think her parents would ever forgive her for running off with Dad. She didn't feel she had anyone to turn to."

"But she did. Your grandparents are letting you live with them. They must care about you."

"That's right, but it wasn't until I landed in jail and the juvenile officer called my grandpa that we all got back together. Grandpa loves Mom, but I think he hates my dad."

"Where's your mom now?"

"Back with him. Can you believe it?"

"Maybe she loves him."

"If that's love, I don't want anything to do with it."

"Is he always that way?"

"No. Sometimes he's fine. Then something sets him off and he goes crazy. It's been worse since I've been in high school. Grandma says he's jealous of me. And Mom says he's a lot better when I'm not around, so I'm living here and they're in the city."

"Do you miss them?"

"My mom and my sister Stacy. But not him."

"How's living with your grandparents?"

"Okay. Better all the time actually. The more

Grandpa sees I'm not like my dad, the better things are."

"And your grandma?"

"She's great. I'd like you to come over and meet them. Would you do that sometime?"

"Sure." If Trent wanted me to meet his grandparents, then we did have a future. And the stories were beginning to make sense now. As usual the rumors held only partial truth.

"What started this fight?"

"It was the Fourth of July. I'd played in the all-star baseball game and won a trophy for most valuable player. Mom and Stacy were at the game. Mom was real proud of me. After the game she took pictures of me with my trophy. Then she and Stacy went home with my trophy. I went to the party the coach threw for the team."

"Your dad wasn't at the game?"

"No. He never went to any of my games. Said they were boring. The truth is he resents the fact that I'm good at baseball. A couple of schools have even talked to me about baseball scholarships. When he heard that he really got mad. Mom said he was a real good baseball player when he was young. He wanted to play pro ball, but never got a chance. Couldn't afford to go to college. He had to work, so he never got the experience or exposure he needed."

"But you're getting the chance he never had. I'd think he'd be glad you could do something he couldn't."

"Some parents might be glad. Not my dad. That night I got home about midnight and he was sitting in the kitchen. My trophy was sitting in front of him. He was staring at it. He didn't hear me come in. I startled him, I guess. I asked him if he liked the trophy. He laughed and told me it was a piece of garbage tin for a piece of garbage kid. Then he lifted the trophy over his head and threw it against the kitchen sink. I walked over and picked it up. I was furious he'd done that. But I was more hurt by what he said about me.''

''Was he drunk or something?'' I knew some people got real crazy when they drank. I thought maybe that was part of his dad's problem.

''No, he wasn't. I used to wish he did drink, then I'd have an excuse for his behavior. He was sober. My mom heard the noise and came into the kitchen. She looked at me holding the trophy and asked what happened. I shrugged my shoulders and started to walk out of the kitchen. I just wanted to get away from him. But that wasn't all right with him.

''He kept screaming at me, telling me I couldn't leave the room without his permission. He loved that, letting me know he had power over me. My mom begged him to leave me alone; I think she knew we were both near the breaking point and was afraid of what might happen. So he turned on her and told her to stay out of it. But she wouldn't. She told him that if he didn't have the decency to be happy for me, at least he should have the decency to leave me alone. I was so proud of her; it was the first time I'd ever heard her stand up to him. But of course that got him even madder.

''He was really shrieking now, going on about how he provided a home for me—ha, some home— and how he was tired of listening to her go on all the time about how wonderful I was. It was her telling him what to do that really had him going now.

''I pleaded with him to let me go to bed. I just wanted to get out of there so he'd let up on Mom. I

113

started toward the door, but he jumped up from his chair, grabbed my shoulder, swung me around, and hissed at me through clenched teeth, 'Don't you ever walk away from me when I'm talking to you.' As if what he'd been doing was talking!

"I pushed his hand off me. I was tired and angry and hurt. But pushing him away just made him even more angry.

" 'You know what you are?' he yelled at me. 'Nothing but a pain in the butt piece of garbage. From the beginning that's all you were. If it wasn't for you, I wouldn't be stuck here.'

"Now my mom was screaming, 'That's enough!'

"But there was no stopping him now. He lit into her, 'I told you to stay out of it. You know as well as I do, the only reason we got married is because you got knocked up.'

"My mother was horrified. She was crying and apologizing to me. I felt sick to my stomach. It wasn't that the news was a shock. After all, I can count. I knew when I was born and when my parents got married. What hurt was seeing how his cruelty had crushed my mother. 'But we loved you. We wanted you,' she kept saying. Maybe she did, but not him. That was pretty clear.

"Now that he'd destroyed my mother, he went back to me. 'What's it to you?' he asked. 'You got a place to sleep, food on the table. That's more than I had at your age. I was out working full-time when I was sixteen.'

"I'd heard this a hundred times before and didn't particularly want to hear it again, and I told him so. That was a mistake. 'And I'll tell you a hundred more times if I want,' he said. 'Sit down.' He tried to push me toward a kitchen chair, but I pushed his hand away again.

114

"Now my mom had recovered a bit, and she stepped in front of me. She was pleading with both of us—him to leave me alone, me to get out of the room. He shoved her hard, so hard she fell against the table and knocked a chair over. I reached for her and he shoved her again. That's when I really started to lose control. It was awful. I couldn't stop yelling at him, but the more I yelled, the more abusive he got, to me and my mom. 'You're just like your mother,' he said to me at one point. 'Good for nothing, the two of you.' That did it for me.

" 'You're the one who's good for nothing,' I told him. 'You're the one who's always complaining and moaning, telling me what a pain in the butt I am. You're the biggest pain of all. Always blaming someone else for your trouble. You're just jealous of me and everyone knows it.'

"That's when he grabbed my trophy out of my hand, screaming, 'Jealous of a punk like you? That's a laugh. Me jealous of a kid who thinks it's the big time bringing home a piece of garbage trophy?' He threw the trophy against the sink again, only this time it bounced off the porcelain and broke in two.

"Mom rushed over to the sink and picked up the pieces. Dad grabbed them out of her hands and flung them to the floor. Then he turned on her and hit her in the face with the back of his hand. When he raised his other clenched fist, I grabbed him from behind. He jerked around and started swinging. I can't remember what happened then except trying not to get hurt too much. He's a big guy but not as tough as he thinks he is. It took two neighbors to pull me off him."

"Oh, Trent." There were tears in my eyes.

"And then you know what the jerk did? He told

115

the policemen who came that I was dangerous and to get me out of his house. Said he wasn't going to have a maniac kid like me around anymore. They kept me in jail for two days trying to find a temporary home for me. Finally the social worker called my grandparents. I'm so glad my grandparents came through. They came down right away to get me out of that awful cell. They talked Mom into coming back here too, but she didn't last long. Why she stays with him is beyond me."

"Oh, Trent, I'm so sorry." I reached over and touched his arm.

"But my grandparents have been real good about it. Grandpa said he doesn't approve of physical violence, but he is proud of me for defending my mother. I like him for telling me that."

"And I bet he likes you, too."

"Yeah, I think he does. He let me have his car again tonight."

"I noticed. Pretty fancy."

"It's okay. As long as it runs, that's all that matters to me."

"Me too." I smiled to myself, hoping his grandfather would let him use it a lot.

"I didn't even know you played baseball." It seemed the safest aspect of Trent's story to focus on.

"Yeah, actually I'm a pretty good second baseman. But after the fight with my father I'm not sure I want to play again this spring."

"But if you're so good and colleges are interested in you, you should play."

"Maybe. I'll see."

"What schools want you?" I was afraid they were a long way from here and I'd never get to see him again. I couldn't believe I was thinking about that.

"State and a private college in Iowa."

"State? Maybe you could join the same fraternity as Brian."

"Right. He'd love that, wouldn't he?"

"He sure would."

We laughed at the idea. And then Trent reached over, put his arm around me and pulled me toward him.

"I'm glad you told me what happened," I said to him.

"I'm glad I told you, too. It's been so hard keeping it all inside, especially after Renee let the story out. I just wanted to scream at her to shut up."

"So did I. I don't know how you managed to be so calm."

"I wasn't inside, believe me."

"You looked pretty calm."

"It was a front. But it's better now. I have no idea what the kids are thinking, but now that you know the truth, I feel okay."

Then he leaned over and kissed me. I put my arms around his neck and kissed him back with all the tenderness I had stored inside me.

Chapter 13

When I got home, Mom was sitting in the kitchen drinking tea. Dad had already gone to bed.

"How was your evening?" Mom asked.

"Good. How come you're still up?"

"I was waiting for you. Want some tea?"

"Sure." I was glad Mom had waited up for me. We've had some of our best talks sitting at the kitchen table sipping tea together.

"Your father told me the rumors about Trent and his family."

"I figured he knew more than he was saying."

"They are rumors, aren't they?"

"I don't know what you heard, Mom." I dreaded telling her Trent had been in jail for hitting his father, but I hoped she'd understand after she knew the whole story.

"Your dad heard Trent beat up his father and that his grandfather had to bail him out of jail."

"Well"—I hesitated—"Trent did get into a fight with his dad. But his dad started it." I gave Mom a brief sketch of what Trent had told me.

"What an awful story."

"And his mom is back living with him. Why would she do that, Mom?"

118

"I don't know, Jeannie. It's hard to know what happens between two people. I suppose she loves him."

"If that's love, I don't want to have anything to do with it." I heard myself echoing Trent's words.

"People sometimes do strange things when they love someone. You know that."

"I sure did." I thought about what I'd done for Sam. I'd run out in the middle of the street with a car coming right at me to stop him from getting hurt.

"How are the kids at school treating Trent?" Mom asked.

"Like the plague. No thanks to Renee."

"Renee?"

"Yeah, she's the one who started all these stories. She wants to get back at both of us. It's so unfair! It's Brian she cares about, not Trent. I wish she'd realize who's really causing her so much pain."

"She will. Just give her time. You've been friends too long to have your friendship end like this."

"I hope so. I really miss her, Mom."

"I'm sure you do." Mom reached over and patted my head. We sat quietly for a few minutes, but I felt how much Mom was with me.

"Tom called tonight. I wanted to talk to you about all of us going to see him next weekend. It's parents' weekend, remember?"

"Yeah, I know, but I don't think I can get off work, Mom. Mr. Nolan is already shorthanded."

"I was afraid of that. I was thinking that if Dad and I went Saturday maybe Renee could stay here Saturday night with you, but now I guess that's out of the question."

"I'm afraid so. But don't worry about me. I'll be fine. I'm old enough to stay by myself."

"Are you sure?"

"Yes, Mom, I'm positive. I'll be fine. Really." I had never stayed alone before, but I could manage it. It might even be nice for a change. If I got lonesome, Trent could come over. That idea was very appealing. I smiled thinking about it.

The next morning Trent was waiting for me by my locker. His face had a lot more color than the night before.

"You're looking good," I said.

"I feel so much better. Thanks for listening last night. Unloading my problems on you really helped."

"I'm glad." We looked at each other. I hoped he could feel how much I cared for him.

"Want to walk me to class?" I slammed my locker door.

"Sure. Say, isn't Jeb in your first-hour class?"

"Yeah, why?"

"I told my grandpa about what a whiz he is with cars. He'd like Jeb to come look at the Packard. Thought I'd tell him."

"He'll like that. You know Jeb is really a good guy once you get beyond the tough facade."

"Aren't we all?" Trent laughed.

"Some of us are just a little tougher than others," I answered.

Jeb wasn't in the room, so we waited near the door. Kids saw us together, but no one commented. I was glad. Maybe the rumors would die out soon and we could get on with our lives.

When Jeb finally showed up a couple of minutes before the bell, he looked tired.

"Hey, Jeb, how's it going?" Trent said.

"Okay. What are you doing here? Don't you have class this hour?"

"Yeah, but I was waiting for you. I was wondering if you'd come over sometime and look at my grandpa's car."

"Sure. Sorry I was so rude when you suggested that before."

"No problem."

"How about Monday when I get off work?"

"Sounds good. Here's the address." Trent scribbled on a slip of paper.

"You better go or you'll be late for class," I said.

"I know. See you at lunch."

The week passed quickly. I spent every free moment with Trent. Being with him made me so happy. He was easy and fun to be with.

After work Wednesday he picked me up and we stopped at McDonald's for a Coke. Trent talked more about his family, and I told him how Sam and I met. It felt good to be able to share my memories of Sam with someone who cared about me.

I hated not being able to share how I felt about Trent with Renee. Every night I wanted to call her and talk. I'd always shared my secrets with Renee; keeping everything inside was so hard.

On Sunday, the car wash was jammed. The mild weather encouraged tons of people to get their cars washed and vacuumed. Jeb's dad was doing pretty well. So far he'd been on time every day and worked hard. He hung around the office when he wasn't busy on the line and asked lots of questions.

"You have quite a job for someone your age."

"I guess so."

"You do the scheduling and payroll?"

"Just the preliminary work." Sometimes I did all the work, but I didn't think that was any of his business.

"I noticed you locked up last Wednesday. You do that often?"

"Sometimes." He seemed awfully curious about everything. I mentioned it to Mr. Nolan.

"Earl Mitchell has been asking me a lot of questions."

"Yeah, he's been doing the same thing with me. Says he wants to know how things are run around here. I like that about him."

"You do?"

"I sure do. I'm looking for someone who can take over when I'm not here. I'd like to start taking a little more time off. Go on a vacation or two this winter. I guess I'm going to need someone here in the office pretty soon, too. You're going off to college next year, and it's not going to be easy to find somebody to do the good job you do."

His compliment pleased me. "But that won't be until next fall."

"I know. Anyway, I've been thinking maybe Earl will work out as assistant manager. It would take a real load off my back to have somebody around here I could trust besides you."

"So it's all right if I answer his questions?"

"Sure."

Earl hung around the booth whenever he wasn't busy on the line. In spite of Mr. Nolan's permission to answer Earl, something about his questions bothered me. I avoided him as much as possible. Near closing time I saw him take a swig out of a brown bag. Mr. Nolan wouldn't like that, but I decided not to snitch. Let Mr. Nolan find out himself about Earl's drinking.

Trent picked me up after work and suggested a fall picnic. He'd packed a blanket, fried chicken, chips, soda, chocolate chip cookies, and a lantern. We found a great spot by a creek. Many of the leaves had already fallen and there was a real autumn feeling in the air.

When I got home Mom called from the living room.

"Brian Gardner wants you to call him. The number is on the refrigerator."

"Brian? Are you serious?"

"Yes. He said he'd be at that number all night."

"I wonder what he wants." Now was my chance to talk to him and see if I could help get him and Renee back together.

"Only one way to find out. Call."

After slipping into my nightgown, I closed my bedroom door and dialed his number.

"Hello, Brian, it's Jeannie."

"Oh, Jeannie. Hi. Thanks for calling me back. I really want to talk to you."

"About what?"

"About Renee. I'm worried about her."

"What do you mean?"

"She won't return my calls. She won't talk to me. Is she all right?"

"As far as I know." For some reason I didn't want to tell Brian that Renee and I weren't speaking.

"Does she ever talk about me?"

"Do you mean does she say anything good about you?"

"That bad, huh?"

"What do you expect?"

He didn't answer that.

"Brian, did you call just to find out if Renee is all right? You could ask her mother that."

"I know. I guess I just want to know if you think there's any chance she and I could get back together."

"What happened to Sandy?"

"Nothing. She's still here."

"Wearing your fraternity pin?"

"No."

"You still dating her."

"Sometimes."

"Tell me, Brian. Do you really think it's all right to have a steady girl there and another here at home?"

"No. I know I screwed up, but it's Renee I care about, not Sandy."

"Then maybe you better tell that to Renee, not me." All along my instincts had been on target. Renee was the girl he loved.

"But she won't even speak to me. I thought maybe you could help me."

"No way, Brian. You want her to know you care about her, you tell her. Be a man and face up to what you did."

"You think she'll forgive me?"

"I don't know. Should she?"

"Yes, because I love her. I really do."

"You had a strange way of showing her that when you brought Sandy for Homecoming."

"I asked Renee. She turned me down."

"She did?" Renee hadn't told me Brian asked her to the dance.

"Yes. Said she already had a date."

"With Trent." Renee could have canceled her date with Trent if she'd wanted to. But she'd been more interested in revenge.

"Right. Jeannie, does she really like that guy?"

"I'm not sure, Brian. You know you should be asking Renee these questions, not me."

"But you're her best friend. She listens to you. I thought maybe you could talk to her for me."

"Brian, listen. Personally, I think she wants you back, but she's hurt and embarrassed. If you really want her back, you'll have to convince her you care about her and nobody else. If you mean it, you might have a chance."

"But how? How can I convince her to see me if she won't even talk to me?"

"I don't know, Brian, but you'll have to think of something."

"I do have one idea. Our game this week is on Friday, so I can come home Saturday night. I was thinking maybe you would set up something so I could see her."

"I don't think so. You should set up your own meeting."

"Please. Invite her to your house Saturday night, and then when she gets there I'll be there."

"What if she doesn't come or won't talk to you?"

"She'll be there if you ask her. And I'll take the chance of getting her to talk to me once I'm with her. Please, Jeannie."

"I suppose I could try. But, Brian, I'm not even sure I can get her to my house."

"Sure you can. I'll see you Saturday, then."

When I hung up, I flopped on my bed. Shoot!

125

Why did I agree to do that? Renee wasn't even speaking to me. How would I ever convince her to come to my house Saturday? Renee was so stubborn sometimes. But Brian was right. Unless he could corral her somewhere alone, she'd never talk to him. I wasn't surprised she refused to take his calls. She didn't want to hear what Trent and I had to say, either. Good thing I had a week to think about it. Maybe Trent and I could come up with a plan.

Chapter 14

Monday morning I told Trent about Brian's call.

"Maybe the guy isn't so bad after all. Did he sound sincere about wanting to patch things up with Renee?" Trent asked.

"Yeah, he did. If only Renee weren't so stubborn."

"How are you going to get her to your house Saturday?"

"I don't know. My parents are going to visit Tom this weekend, and Mom suggested I invite Renee to stay with me. Normally that would have been a fine idea, but now she wouldn't even consider it. You got any ideas?"

"Not at the moment. But let's think about it. One of us is bound to get a brainstorm."

"I hope so."

Renee passed me in the halls a couple of times. The first time I said hello and smiled, I caught her by surprise. For a second there was a flicker of interest in her eyes, but she caught herself and looked away. The next time she didn't even bother to look at me. I wondered how long it would take for her to break down and talk to me. Even Sheila was starting to be friendly. She at least said hi.

Trent felt the tension ease for him a little, too. I

hoped it would get even better. In one sense we were both so happy having each other that we didn't care too much what everyone else thought. But it was also hard to admit how much it hurt to be ignored.

On Tuesday morning Jeb was in a talkative mood.

"Dad's doing all right at the car wash, huh?"

"Yeah. Mr. Nolan likes him a lot."

"It doesn't pay much though, does it?"

"Minimum wage to start. Your dad got his first check Friday, right?"

"Yeah, and he was kind of depressed about it. Claimed it wasn't near enough for the work he was doing. But he said he'd be bringing home a lot more real soon."

"I'm sure he'll get a raise in a couple of months. If Mr. Nolan likes somebody, that's what he does." I didn't think it would be too much more.

"He told Mom it would be a lot sooner than that."

I shrugged my shoulders. I'd never known Mr. Nolan to give anyone a raise right away, but he really did like Earl, and he had talked about making him assistant manager.

"Does the car wash really take in a couple of thousand on a good weekend?"

"Sometimes."

"Dad can't believe the bucks Nolan makes."

I shrugged again. Mr. Nolan did make good money during the warmer months of the year. Winter was a lot slower.

"The business does all right."

"Must be something to have all that money," Jeb said.

"I guess so," I answered.

"Talk about money. I was over to Trent's place

last night. That's some house they have. You been there?''

"No. How did it go with his grandpa?"

"Pretty good. I was nervous when I first got there, but once we started talking cars, it was easy.''

"Are you going to help him?"

"A little. I gave him some advice on where he could get parts and who to call for suggestions. He seemed to like my advice. Imagine a guy like that listening to someone like me.''

"Jeb, you don't give yourself enough credit. You're a genius when it comes to cars.''

"I'm not a genius, I just like working on them.''

"You're too humble.''

"Anyway, I told him I'd help him out when I had time. He wants to do work himself, but he'd like me to come over when I can to see how he's doing.''

"Is Trent going to help?"

"I doubt it. Trent isn't into cars much. But I'm glad he introduced me to his grandpa.''

"That's Trent. He's really a good guy. He cares a lot about other people.''

"How's he handling all the gossip?"

"Pretty good. He feels bad that the story got out at all. But you know people. They love to talk.''

"They sure do.'' Both of us remembered the rumors people had spread about Sam. "You and Renee speaking yet?''

"No, and somehow I have to get her to my house Saturday night.''

"Why?''

I told him about Brian wanting to make up with Renee.

"Personally, I can't stand the guy. And Renee is not at the top of my list either, but I can see how

129

those two are right for each other," Jeb said. "Good luck."

"Thanks. If you come up with any ideas, let me know."

"Steve and I could kidnap her and dump her on your doorstep."

"No good. I'd prefer she came willingly. Anything less could be disastrous."

All week I tried to think of a way to get Renee to come over. Finally on Friday I decided I'd just confront her even if she refused to talk to me. Before school I waited for her near her locker. I could tell she was surprised to see me. Sheila was trailing her. "I'll catch you later," she said and took off before Renee could object.

"Hi," I said hoping this wasn't going to be as difficult as I feared.

Renee didn't answer me. She opened her locker and started fixing her hair using the mirror inside her locker door.

"Renee, could you stop that a second and talk to me?"

"I don't have anything to say to you." She kept on combing her hair.

"Maybe you don't, but I do. Mom and Dad are going to see Tom this weekend and I wondered if you would stay overnight with me tomorrow night."

That got her attention. "Are you serious?"

"Yes, I am."

"You mean your parents are going to be gone for the whole night and you want me to stay with you?"

"Yes."

"What about you and lover boy, Trent?"

"What about us?"

"I'd think you two lovebirds would relish the idea of an empty house for an entire night."

"Come on, Renee. You know I'm not like that."

"I do? No, I don't. Everytime you fall in love, you act so strange. You don't have time for anybody but the guy. And this time it had to be Trent."

"Will you stay with me?" I wasn't up for an argument.

"Why? So we can fight some more?"

"No, not fight. Talk. I miss you." I looked away, realizing how very much I did miss my best friend.

"Well, I'm busy."

"Please, Renee. I need to talk to you."

"About what? About how it's perfectly all right to steal your best friend's boyfriend and make a fool out of her?"

"I'm sorry about all that. I really am. Maybe if we could talk you'd understand."

"I understand as well as I want to."

"I have to close up tomorrow. Would you at least pick me up and drive me home? If you don't want to spend the night I understand, but we could order a pizza and talk for a while."

"Give it up, Jeannie. We don't have anything to talk about. I have to go." She slammed her locker door and was gone.

Jeb tried to cheer me up when I told him about my talk with Renee. He told me not to worry, things have a way of working themselves out. I wished he were right. This time he wasn't.

During lunch I tried to reach Brian to tell him there was no way I could help him, but he wasn't around. Finally I decided to stop worrying about it. Maybe he could find her at Arly's or the Heights or somewhere.

I'd done my best, and it hadn't worked. Let Brian figure it out for himself.

Friday at work I had trouble balancing. I was off by over fifty dollars. For the third time in a week I couldn't get the books right. Mr. Nolan told me not to worry about it, I could figure it out some other time. I had the nagging suspicion Earl Mitchell had something to do with the missing money, but I kept silent. I needed more than just my intuition to accuse him of stealing.

After work I wandered over to see the last part of the football game. Mostly I wanted to see Trent. After the game I met him at Arly's. I looked for Renee, but she was nowhere around.

Saturday was a super-busy day. Mr. Nolan was going to the cities in the afternoon for a wedding, so he asked me to put the cash in the safe after closing and lock up. I didn't usually do that on Saturday because of all the money involved, but I didn't mind every now and then. Earl was in charge of the line. Mr. Nolan was confident the two of us would manage just fine. He was planning to be back to open on Sunday.

About two o'clock, Mr. Nolan got ready to leave. "It's pretty busy out there. Lots of car washes, but not much pumping gas. I better not complain though, some business is better than none." He looked at the automatic car counter. "Almost 300 cars already, and we still have three hours to go."

"That's great. Earl must be collecting a bundle out there. I think I've only given out about a hundred car wash slips. Hopefully the counter will help me balance tonight."

On busy days or when he wasn't around, Mr. Nolan set the automatic car counter. Knowing the exact number of cars sometimes helped me find my errors.

"I'll see you tomorrow. I'm leaving this number in case you need me. I told Earl it's here, too." He pointed to a telephone number scribbled on the calendar. "Be sure to double-check everything before you leave."

"I will. Have fun."

The last three hours went quickly. At closing time, Earl dumped the money he'd collected on the line on my desk, but the numbers didn't agree. The money I had accounted for 310 cars, but by five o'clock the counter read 393. My suspicions of Earl were being confirmed.

Between worrying about the possible theft and Renee, I was a nervous wreck. Brian was going to show up at my house and Renee wasn't going to be there. I kept hoping Renee would change her mind and show up to drive me home. The only bright spot was that Trent was coming over around seven.

With the entrance closed, the crew quickly finished the cars already in line. Earl was in a good mood. His enthusiasm helped the men get the cars out fast. I tried again to balance. I rechecked the counter. It read 393. This was the same problem I'd had on Wednesday. But this time there was a discrepancy of 83 cars. I was over $200 short.

Earl opened the door.

"We're done out here. How you doing?"

"Fair."

"Why the frown? You having problems?"

"Not exactly. I was just thinking about something else."

"Probably that boy who comes around here."

I smiled. "Busy day out there," I said.

"Yeah, it sure was. A little over 300 cars."

"Closer to 400. Now if I could only get the money to agree." How stupid did he think we were? Maybe if he realized I knew he was stealing, he'd put the money back.

"Four hundred? No way. I kept real good track of the cars today. Just over 300."

"My count says 393." I looked up at him. His eyes were black and piercing and bloodshot.

"Well, you counted wrong." He pulled the ledger from me. "Let me see this."

"Hey, what are you doing?" I stood up and pulled it from his hands. "I think you better just let me do my work and you do yours." At that moment I realized I shouldn't have tipped my hand. Mr. Nolan was the person to deal with Earl, not me. We had the automatic counter as proof, and apparently Earl didn't know it existed. I wasn't about to tell him.

He let me take the book, but he gave me the most frightening look. "Like I said, I counted real carefully today. It's 310. He pulled a small notebook from his pocket and dropped it on my desk. "You saying I'm wrong?"

"No, I'm not. I'm sure you're right." I opened my ledger and began working. I didn't want him to see my face. The shortage problem this week was confirmed. Jeb's dad was stealing. I didn't know what to say or do. He turned his back to me and I saw him shove the calendar with Mr. Nolan's number in his coat.

"Want me to help you finish up?" Earl offered.

"No, no, it's my job. I'm about done," I stammered. Now that I was certain he was guilty, I wasn't sure what to do.

"Let me put the money in the safe."

"No, I'll do it. Why don't you just go on and lock up out there?" My hands were shaking. I had to get out of there. Fear filled the pit of my stomach.

"I'll wait. I want to be sure we understand each other. See, Jeannie, I counted those cars real good today—310." Something in his voice frightened me. I knew I had to agree with him.

"Yeah, you're right," I stammered. "I see my error now. It's right here."

"You sure?" He tried to see what I was doing.

"I got it, really." I slammed the book shut. I'd come back later and finish. Right now I just wanted him away from me. I was certain I smelled whiskey on his breath. His eyes were glazed. I understand the fear Jeb must have felt when his dad got angry.

"Tell me the combination. I'll do it." He turned to me, waiting for an answer.

"I don't use a combination."

He came toward me. I wanted to scream.

There was a loud tapping on the glass. "You need a ride or not?" Renee leaned against the door.

"Yeah, I sure do, Renee. Come on in. I was just finishing up."

"Well, hurry up, will you?"

Never in my life was I so glad to see Renee. Earl looked at her, then me.

"You're sure about the money?" he asked.

"I'm sure. See, 310 cars, just like you said, and money for the same number." I pointed toward the book. "I'll see you tomorrow." My mind was racing. Earl was stealing, and today it had been at least $200. My heart ached for Jeb. What was I going to do?

"What's the matter?" Renee asked. "You so surprised to see me you turn pale?"

"No, it's not because of you. That guy gives me the creeps." In the old days I would have told Renee what had frightened me, but these days I wasn't sure I could trust her. I didn't want her spreading rumors about Jeb and his family.

"Isn't that Jeb Mitchell's dad?"

"Yeah, he's been working here for a couple of weeks."

"He's three sheets to the wind. Where's the boss?"

"At a wedding."

"Ah, when the boss is away the mouse will play."

"Yup." He sure did play, too. That explained him telling Jeb's mom that he'd have more money soon. He was planning all along to steal from the car wash.

"I sure am glad to see you. Let's go." I was so relieved to lock up and get out of there. Earl hadn't left. He watched my every move. I rechecked the alarm system and hurried to Renee's car. I was still shaking.

"So what's this big emergency you needed to talk to me about?" Renee pulled away from the car wash and sped toward my house. I'd been so frightened by Jeb's dad I'd forgotten about Brian. Oh, no! Why had I ever put myself into this position? Finally Renee was talking to me and I was about to deceive her.

"You talk to Brian lately?" I asked.

"No, and I don't ever intend to speak to that slimeball again."

"Come on, Renee. You know you still love the guy. Talk to him."

"Is that what you want to talk to me about? If it is, forget it. The last thing I need from you is advice about guys."

"Renee, give me a break. I've had a hard day."

136

"And I've had a hard month. If you expect me to tell you everything is all right, forget it. It's not."

"I don't expect you to say everything is all right. But it would be nice if you listened to someone else for a change. There are two sides to every story, even yours and Brian's."

"So you wanted to see me to give me a lecture."

"Maybe I did. I've had it." My frustration and fear all came spilling out. "You're acting like a spoiled brat and since no one else has the guts to tell you, I'm going to. Sure, Brian acted like a real jerk. But you never gave him a chance to apologize. Every time he tried, you flew off the handle and refused to listen. You wouldn't even go to the Homecoming dance with him when he asked you.

"And then you did the same thing to Trent and me when you saw us at the car wash. If we could have all sat down and talked things out, maybe none of this would have happened. But you're too busy blaming everybody else for your problems to listen to the other side."

"You don't know what you're talking about."

"Oh, yes, I do. And so do you, if you'd just be honest. But the worst part was how you spread those rumors about Trent and his family. That was a terrible, mean, cruel thing to do. He's trying to start over and he didn't need you causing any more trouble. And me? I'm your best friend. I never stole Trent from you, and we both know it. He wasn't yours in the first place. You only wanted him for what he could do for you, to make Brian jealous. I want Trent because of who he is. And I need you to be happy for me. If you can't manage to forgive a little, then I give up. I don't want you for a friend if you can't at least try.

"And on top of everything else right now, I have to figure out what I'm going to do about Jeb's dad. I know he stole money today, and he knows I know, and I'm scared to death. So I don't need you or anyone else giving me a hard time."

I was just about out of steam when we arrived at my house. Brian was already there. "In case you're wondering, yes, that's Brian's car. Like a fool I agreed to try and get you two back together. If you want to talk to him, fine. If you don't, that's fine, too. This is the last time I'm doing anything for either one of you. Now if you'll excuse me, I'm going in." I jumped out of her car and slammed the door.

Brian had gotten out of his car when we pulled up. I turned on him.

"And as for you, Brian Gardner, you're a real jerk. I'm not sure myself if I'd forgive you." I stormed past him into the house. I flopped on the couch and sank into the cushions. At that moment I didn't care about anyone or anything.

Chapter 15

I didn't move from the couch for a long time. When I finally got up to get a soda, Brian and Renee and both their cars were gone. I had no idea what happened to them, but my thoughts were less on them than on Earl Mitchell. Part of me was very afraid. That man was vicious when he was drunk. How many times had Jeb told me that?

When the doorbell rang at 7:30, I was so happy to see Trent I grabbed him around the neck and hugged him tight.

"Wow, that's some greeting."

"I'm so glad to see you." As I closed the door behind Trent, I saw a car turn down my block that looked like Earl's. My stomach was in knots.

Trent listened to the whole story.

"Maybe you should call the police."

"And what am I going to say? I don't have actual proof he stole the money. Just the numbers on the counter. If only Mr. Nolan were here."

"Can't you get ahold of him?"

"He left a number on the calendar on the bulletin board, but Earl took it. He shoved it in his coat and I have no idea what the number was."

"Do you remember at all where he said the wedding was?"

"No, just that it's in Minneapolis. I tried calling his house, but all I got was his answering machine. Oh, Trent, what am I going to do?"

"Do you really think he'll try something?"

"I don't know. I've heard stories from Jeb for years about how crazy his dad gets when he's drinking."

"Maybe we should call Jeb."

"I was thinking that. But what would I say? 'Your dad's a thief'?"

"That would be rough, but Jeb's had a lot of experience handling his dad. He might have some ideas about what to do."

"I suppose it's worth a try." I dailed Jeb's number, but there was no answer. "Saturday night. He's probably out with the guys."

"Try his work number."

"Nobody there either," I said after dialing it.

I looked out the window, afraid I'd see Earl again. No cars were on the street. Trent's grandpa's car wasn't either. "You walked, huh?"

"Yeah. Grandma and Grandpa went out to dinner."

"Think we should walk over to Arly's? Maybe Jeb is there."

"That's a long way if he's not."

"I know, but at least we'd be doing something." I fought to curb the panic creeping through me.

"Better take a coat. It's getting cold."

We walked the two miles quickly. Not much was going on at Arly's. Renee was nowhere to be found. Neither was Brian. I didn't know if that was a good sign or not. I asked a few kids if they'd seen Jeb, but nobody had. I told them to tell him I was looking for him if they ran into him.

About ten o'clock we decided to walk home.

We were about a block from Arly's when a car began to inch along beside us. I recognized Earl Mitchell behind the wheel.

"Maybe we should go back to Arly's and ask somebody for a ride," I suggested, realizing how foolish it had been to set out alone on foot.

We turned around and hurried toward Arly's. It took Earl a little while to figure out what we were doing. We were almost to the parking lot when he pulled alongside us and jumped out.

"I want to talk to you." Earl motioned to me. His eyes were bloodshot and his speech slurred.

"About what?" I stammered.

"You know about what." He waved to Trent. "Take a walk, boy."

"I'm not going anywhere. And Jeannie doesn't want to talk to you, so why don't you just leave."

"You talking to me, boy?"

"Yes, I am. Come on Jeannie, let's go." Trent clutched my hand and we started toward Arly's.

"Hey, I want to talk to you." He came up behind me and grabbed my arm.

"Take your hands off her." Trent pushed Earl's hand from me.

"Get lost, kid." Earl's voice was low and threatening. The smell of whiskey was everywhere on him.

"No, you're the one leaving." Trent stepped in front of me. My heart raced. I was so afraid I could barely breathe.

"Get out of the way. You don't scare me. I got a son who thinks he's a hotshot just like you." He shoved the index finger of his right hand into Trent's chest.

"Keep your hands off me." Trent pushed his finger away.

"Just like you." He shoved his left hand into Trent's chest. Trent pushed it away a second time. But Earl came back with his right fist and smashed Trent square on the jaw. Trent stumbled backwards.

I screamed. Before Trent could get up, Earl fell on him and struck him a second time in the face. I tried to pull him off Trent. Trent finally managed to heave Earl off him. They rolled over and Trent pinned Earl's arms to the ground so he couldn't hit him anymore. By this time kids from Arly's surrounded us.

Jeb emerged from the crowd.

"What's going on?" Jeb yelled. He grabbed Trent around the neck and pulled him off his father.

"Take it easy, Jeb. Let me explain," Trent tried to reason with Jeb.

Jeb wouldn't listen. "You can beat up your old man, but you leave mine alone." He squeezed Trent's neck tighter.

I pounded on Jeb's arm. "Let him go. Let him go."

Jeb's father struggled to his feet and staggered toward the car. He reached into the front seat, pulled out a bottle, and took a drink.

"You're going to jail, you punk. You tried to kill me," Earl screamed at Trent.

"That's not true," I cried. "You started it."

Sirens filled the air. Someone at Arly's must have called the police.

Jeb still had Trent in a headlock. Two policemen jumped out of a squad car, billy clubs in their hands.

"What's going on here?" one of them asked.

"He jumped me," Earl pointed at Trent.

The policeman turned to Jeb and Trent.

"When I got here, he was on top of my dad," Jeb said.

"Let him go," the policeman said. Jeb released Trent.

"Put your hands on top of the car and spread your legs." The policeman searched Trent for weapons.

"That's not true. He started it." I pointed to Jeb's dad. "Jeb, listen to me."

Jeb looked down at me.

"That little punk tried to kill me," Earl muttered.

"Well, you're awfully quiet. What do you have to say for yourself?" the policeman asked Trent.

"He was harrassing her. I told him to leave her alone. He wouldn't."

"I work with her. I needed to talk to her, and he wouldn't let me. He's crazy, I'm telling you," Earl insisted.

"Do you work with him?" the policeman asked me.

"Yes, but Trent's—"

"See, what did I tell you?" Earl interrupted me.

"Did you hit him?" The policeman questioned Trent.

"I pinned him to the ground."

"So Earl wouldn't hit him again," I tried to tell the policeman.

"Did you strike the kid?" The policeman turned to Earl.

"I want this punk in jail, you hear me."

"Are you saying you want to press charges against him?"

"You bet I do."

143

"Get in." The policeman opened the back seat of the squad car. "That your car?" he asked Earl.

Earl nodded.

"Follow us to the station. We'll discuss this down there. The rest of you go on back to whatever you were doing."

I looked at Trent. He looked defeated and scared. I wanted to cry. I didn't understand why he didn't try to defend himself.

The squad car pulled away and Jeb's dad followed. I raced to Jeb's car.

"Jeb, you've got to listen to me."

"I'm listening, but I'm not sure I want to."

"Your father started this. He hit Trent first."

"Why would my old man start a fight with Trent? That makes no sense, Jeannie."

"It will when you listen to me. There's something I have to tell you. I didn't want to say it in front of the police officers."

"What?"

"Take me to the police station. We'll talk on the way. Please," I pleaded.

"All right."

I got into his car.

"Does this have anything to do with why you've been looking for me?" Jeb asked.

"Yes. Jeb, your father is stealing money from the car wash."

"What?"

"We've been short four days this week. At first I thought maybe it was my mistake, but today I found out it wasn't. Your dad is pocketing some of the money he collects on the line."

"He wouldn't be that stupid. You're just trying to get your boyfriend off the hook."

"It's true, Jeb. Think about it. I bet your dad had extra money this week, didn't he?"

Jeb didn't answer. He wouldn't look at me, either.

"Your father was following me because today he knew I figured it out. He wanted to talk to me alone, and Trent said no. He shoved his finger in Trent's chest and then hit him. I swear, Jeb, that's the truth."

"My dad may be a drunk, but a thief? I don't want to believe that."

"I know you don't, Jeb. But people do crazy things when they're desperate. It's not right, but it happens. You're not helping your dad if you ignore this."

"How do I know you're telling the truth? Maybe you took the money yourself for Trent, and now you want to blame my old man."

"Jeb, you know better."

There was a long awkward silence. I knew Jeb was struggling with himself, trying to find a way to avoid facing the painful truth. "I don't know," he finally said. "All I know is I saw Trent on top of my old man. I need to be by myself for a while. Maybe you should just get out."

He pulled to the curb. I felt sick to my stomach. I opened the door and stepped out. "Jeb, please, believe me," I pleaded. He pulled away without answering.

I walked the rest of the way to the police station. I wasn't sure what I would do when I got there. I didn't want to tangle with Jeb's dad. That much I knew.

Earl's car was still at the station. At the door I peeked in. Earl was leaning against the wall. I could see the paper bag in his back pocket. Trent was nowhere in sight. I was desperate to find out what

145

had happened to Trent, but I was afraid to face Earl. Hating myself for my cowardice, I crept away.

But I knew I had to help Trent. I walked back to the Seven-Eleven and called his grandparents. Nobody answered. I had no idea who their friends were. Why did Mom and Dad pick today of all days to be out of town? And Mr. Nolan, too. I called his house and left another message on his answering machine.

Upset, afraid, and angry, I decided to go home. I kept an eye out for Jeb's dad, but didn't see him anywhere.

At home I kept calling Trent's grandparents, but no one answered. I called the motel where my parents were staying, but they were still out. Around midnight I heard a car. I peeked out the living room window and my heart sank. It was Earl Mitchell. I checked all the locks and pretended I didn't hear the doorbell. It rang and rang. Then he started pounding on the door. The man was crazy. If I pretended not to be here, maybe he'd go away. Did he know my parents were out of town? At last the knocking stopped. I looked out again and he was getting back into his car. Just then I saw Trent walking down the street. I was so relieved, but scared too. What would happen when Trent saw Earl?

I opened the froot door just a crack, but left the chain attached.

"What are you doing here?" Trent asked as he approached Earl.

"Listen, punk, those stupid cops let you go this time, but next time I'll make sure they lock you up and throw away the key. Now get out of the way. I have something to settle with Miss Goodie Two Shoes."

"She has nothing to say to you, so I suggest you

get out of here before she calls the police. Unless of course you want her talking to them.''

"You don't scare me.''

"And you don't scare me. The sergeant on duty told you to go home and sober up. He won't be happy to hear you're over here causing trouble.''

"You little punk." He took another step toward Trent. Trent held his ground.

"Now get out of here," Trent said. Earl staggered a little and then turned toward his car. Before he reached it, Jeb pulled up to the curb. I yanked the chain from the latch and raced to Trent.

"You all right?" Trent asked me.

"I'm okay. Are you?''

"Yes.''

"I've been calling your grandparents. No answer.''

"I know. But it's all right. It didn't take the desk sergeant long to figure out this guy was loaded and looking for a fight.''

Jeb jumped out of his car and walked toward his dad.

"What are you doing here, Dad?''

"Came to talk to her. Set her straight." Earl pointed toward me.

"About what?" Jeb asked him.

"About my job, if it's any of your business, which it ain't.''

"I just came from Jack's Bar. Ma is there having one fine time.''

"Good for her. I think I'll join her.''

"She was flashing this around." Jeb held up a wad of bills. "She said you gave them to her.''

"That's right, I did.''

"Where'd you get this?''

"I got paid yesterday.''

"Not this much, Dad."

"How do you know what I get paid?"

"I can guess. And I know it can't be this much."

"Give me those." He reached for the bills. Jeb pulled them away.

"I said give me those, you little snot."

"No, Dad. I won't. You took this money from the car wash. Maybe if you agree to give it back, Mr. Nolan won't throw you in jail."

"That fool has so much money he won't even miss it. If that little Miss Goodie Two Shoes just keeps her mouth shut, nobody needs to know."

"Oh, so Jeannie should lie for you so you can go back tomorrow and steal some more."

"Look who's talking? You and your high and mighty principles. Look around you, boy, we have nothing but trouble. I work my butt off day after day for nothing. Well, not anymore I ain't. No, sirree."

He tried again to grab the money from Jeb. Jeb yanked it away a second time and stuffed it in his pocket.

"You're disgusting."

"Give me that." He lunged for Jeb. Jeb stepped aside, but he clenched his fists ready to strike.

"Don't do it, Jeb. It isn't worth it, believe me." Trent stepped toward Jeb.

"He's nothing but a drunken bum and a thief," Jeb said through clenched teeth. His fists were raised.

His dad clawed at Jeb's pocket for the money. Trent lowered Jeb's fists. "Let him have it. Fighting with him isn't going to do you any good. I know."

Jeb shoved his father away. Then he pulled the bills from his pocket and threw them at his dad.

"You make me sick, you know that."

Earl scrambled on the ground for the money. Then

he staggered to his car. Jeb watched in total disgust. We all did. When the car pulled away, Trent touched Jeb on the arm. "It'll be all right."

"No it won't." Jeb jerked his arm away from Trent's hand. "No, it won't. My dad's a thief. How can it be all right?"

"I didn't mean it like that, I only meant . . ." Trent tried to calm Jeb down.

Jeb's frustrations came roaring out. He clutched his fists and turned and swung at Trent. Trent grabbed his arm, but didn't swing back. Jeb hit Trent in the chest hard. Trent still didn't respond. Jeb hit him again, a little softer. Tears streamed down his face. The look of empathy and sadness and concern on Trent's face overwhelmed him. I stood helplessly watching a lifetime of frustration pour from Jeb.

"You did the right thing, Jeb. Really." Trent talked to Jeb calmly, quietly.

"I wanted to smash him. I wanted to beat on him for his stupidity." He hit Trent's chest again. He wasn't aware of what he was doing.

"I know. But what good would it do?"

"Maybe I'd feel better."

"And maybe you'd end up in jail, too." Trent let go of Jeb's left hand.

"You're right. But now what? He's going to end up in jail when Mr. Nolan finds out. I have to help him."

"Jeb, you can't cover for your dad forever. He's responsible for his own actions."

"But he's my father. If I don't help him, who will?"

"He'll have to help himself. You've tried to help more than any other kid would. You can't spend your whole life trying to clear the way for him."

"I know, but he's gotten so bad the last few years. Ma, too."

"I know how that is. But you can't take care of them forever. This time your dad got in too deep."

Jeb turned to me. "I'm sorry, Jeannie. His working there was a bad idea. I knew it."

"No, Jeb, it was an okay idea. Your father is the one who blew it, not you."

"Are you going to tell Mr. Nolan?" Jeb looked at me and I wanted to cry.

I nodded my head yes. "I have to."

"I know. Just for a second I was hoping maybe you wouldn't, but you have to. I know that."

"He'll survive, Jeb." Trent reassured him.

"Guess I better not go home tonight," Jeb said.

"You can stay here if you want. I'm sure Mom and Dad wouldn't mind," I offered.

"Thanks. I just might do that."

Lights flashed on the street. Renee's blue Mustang stopped in front of the house.

Chapter 16

When Renee stepped out of her car, I hurried over to stop her from asking embarrassing questions in front of Jeb.

"You look awful. What happened?" Renee asked.

"I don't think I could even begin to explain. What are you doing here anyway?"

"When I heard about the trouble at Arly's, I came right over."

"Why?" I didn't think Renee cared enough anymore to do that.

"To see if you were all right."

"Barely." I was glad she was here, but too drained to show my gratitude.

"What's going on? Jeb looks awful." Renee nodded toward the guys. Even from this distance his distress was obvious.

"Don't start, Renee." I was in no mood to have to defend Jeb once again.

"What does that mean? I just asked a question."

"I know you don't like Jeb, but I do. He's got tons of problems right now, so don't give him a hard time."

"I wasn't going to. The truth is I wanted to thank him."

"You wanted to thank Jeb? For what?"

"For threatening me."

"Threatening you?"

"If it hadn't been for him, I'd never have shown up at the car wash this afternoon."

"You came because of Jeb?" Right now the afternoon seemed a thousand years ago. I couldn't believe only a few hours had passed since the start of all the trouble with Earl Mitchell.

"That's right. Jeb came to my house this afternoon and told me if I didn't come on my own to see you today, he was going to tie me up and drag me here."

"Jeb said that?"

"Yes, he did. He sounded so crazy he scared me. Anyway, he said he was sick and tired of you being so depressed because we were fighting. And he said you were sick and tired of seeing me depressed because of Brian."

"Jeb said that? I don't believe it."

"It's true. I wasn't about to let him drive me anywhere, so I agreed to pick you up from work."

"And I was so out of it because of what was going on with Jeb's dad, I could barely deal with you. I'm sorry I didn't have time to prepare you for Brian."

"Maybe it was better that way. If I'd known Brian was at your house, I probably never would have driven you home."

"So what happened between you and Brian?"

"We had a long talk about why he was dating Sandy and why I went out with Trent. He says he loves me, but he's not ready to commit to me one hundred percent. And I guess I'm not ready, either. I don't want to spend my whole senior year sitting home waiting for him to call. We decided we'd go out with each other when he's home, but date other people this year, too.''

"You went along with that?"

"Yeah, I did. Some part of me loves Brian very much, but I'm also hurt about what he did and how he did it. I'm not ready yet to trust him.''

"Do you think you'll ever be ready to do that again?''

"I don't know. I don't feel as angry at him as I did, so maybe "

"That's a start. Meanwhile, what are you planning to do? You still interested in Trent?'' I dreaded bringing him up, but I had to know how she felt.

"Relax, Jeannie. You were right that I was really just using Trent. And since you and I haven't been speaking, you haven't noticed Tim and I have been spending a lot of time together.''

"You and Tim?"

"Yeah. Does that surprise you?"

"Yeah. I knew Tim liked you, but I never knew he wanted to go out with you. And I sure never knew you thought about going out with him.''

"I didn't, until we began spending so much time together complaining about how miserable we were because we'd both been dumped. Then one day we got tired of sounding like broken records and decided it was time to stop moaning and get on with our lives. We figured we each knew how to have a good time, so why not try having a good time together.''

"Tim and you, huh? I like it.''

"Good. I do, too.''

"But do you still think I stole Trent from you?''

"Well . . .''

"Do you?'' I pressed.

"No, I guess not. I was just so hurt by what Brian

153

did, and then you seemed to be doing the same thing."

"But I wasn't. I tried so hard not to like Trent, but I just couldn't help myself."

"I know. I should have been happy for you instead of giving you a hard time. I'm sorry."

"So am I. I've missed you so much." I reached over and hugged her tight. We both brushed tears from our eyes.

"Let's go in the house." I signaled for the guys to follow us.

Trent paused. He wasn't sure what to do.

"Come on. She won't bite. Right, Renee?"

"Right."

When we reached the front door, Trent put his arm around me and pulled me to him. Renee smiled. Jeb opened the front door and held it for Renee. Trent hesitated on the step. When I looked up at him, he leaned toward me. When his lips brushed mine, I kissed him back and pulled him toward me. As we walked through the front door, I remembered Sam and smiled, knowing he would have approved.